HIDDEN TREASURES

A PINX VIDEO MYSTERY

MARSHALL THORNTON

KENMORE BOOKS

Published by Kenmore Books

Edited by Joan Martinelli

Cover design by Marshall Thornton

Images by 123rf stock

ISBN-13: 978-1983576201

ISBN-10: 1983576204

First Edition

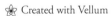 Created with Vellum

ACKNOWLEDGMENTS

I would like to thank Joan Martinelli, Randy and Valerie Trumbull, Kevin E. Davis, Nathan Bay, William Miller, Mark Jewkes and Louis Dumser, Robin Sinclair, and Helene Augustyniak.

1

"ABSOLUTELY NOT," I INSISTED.

It was a Thursday night, my regular night to have dinner with my downstairs neighbors, Marc and Louis. I sometimes had dinner with them on Sundays or Tuesdays or Fridays as well, but that was dependent on everyone's schedule. Thursday was the night we marked down in our Day Runners.

"Oh come on, it'll be fun," their friend Leon said. He was just past forty and liked to dye his spiky hair white-blond.

"You're not the one who ended up hanging off a balcony," I pointed out, sipping a cup of coffee that was more cream and amaretto than coffee. I should have told Louis to hold the amaretto. And the cream. And probably the coffee.

"I'm sure that won't happen again," Leon said. "How about we put a prohibition on tall buildings?"

"How about we put a prohibition on amateur homicide investigations?"

"Well, I want to know," Marc said. "Who's this person who got himself murdered?"

I was tempted to stick my fingers in my ears and sing "lalalalala" so I didn't have to listen. Instead, I looked up at the starless night. Well, it wasn't really starless. The stars were there, it was just that you couldn't see them from Silver Lake—or anywhere else in Los Angeles—since there was always too much light pollution at night. It never really got dark enough to see stars.

"…costume house over on Santa Monica and Mariposa…"

Maybe I should hum. That might block them out. We were sitting in the courtyard of our six-unit, L-shaped, stucco apartment building. It had been painted a stormy gray with bright white trim around the windows and on the railings. The courtyard was crowded with very old plants and we sat under a giant bird-of-paradise that was probably planted there during the Korean War when the building was built. An iron table sat outside Marc and Louis' apartment, so they'd commandeered it on a permanent basis.

"What do you think, Noah?" Louis asked.

"About what?"

"About the costumer who was murdered."

"Did he have a butler?"

"No one has a butler anymore," Marc said.

"Then I have no idea who killed him."

"Ha-ha," Leon said to my joke. Then he went on, "Everyone at the studio is in an uproar. He supplied costumes for nearly half our shows."

"What exactly is a costume house?" Louis asked.

"They collect costumes," I explained. "They're usually headed by a designer, so they make some of the costumes as well."

"Collecting costumes is profitable?"

"It's not collecting like you do with coins or stamps. Although, I guess people do that, too. This is more like Hertz, except for costumes." I was getting a blank stare, so I continued. "Say you're working on a show like *Gunsmoke*—"

"Oh my God, that's not still on the air, is it?" Leon asked.

"No, it's not. Anyway, on a show like that you have to dress all the background people. So you charge the studio whatever it costs to make or buy the costumes for the extras. Then you rent them out to the next Western that comes along and that's where you make your profit."

Why was I explaining this? I was better off looking at the sky.

"So, why kill someone like that?" Marc asked.

"Well…" I stood up. "It's time for me to go upstairs. Everything was delicious, Louis."

"Let me make up a plate for you," he said, jumping up.

"Oh you don't have to."

"Yes, I do!" he called out, already running into the kitchen.

Louis' dinner had been delicious. It was just that delicious had become a more abstract concept than it had once been. It used to mean food that was so good it could not be resisted. Now it was simply something I knew about food, even as I pushed it away.

"Apparently, the police think it was a burglary gone wrong, but they can't find anything missing," Leon said to Marc.

I walked over to the foot of the stairs that led up to the second floor. I did not want to get pulled into their discussion. I'd had enough of people being murdered and wanted nothing to do with it ever, ever again.

Louis popped out of his apartment and came over. He'd actually made me two plates: one with the beef tips and mashed potatoes ("That's potato with an E," he'd said as he'd served them, "in honor of Vice President Quayle."); and the other was fresh, homemade strawberry pie, which he'd served for dessert without political commentary.

"Please don't take offense, I mean this in the nicest way," he began. My stomach sank. Very few good comments began that way. I waited. He said, "You're not a fashion model."

"I know that."

"You don't need to be this thin."

"I have a fast metabolism," I lied.

"Well, maybe this extra piece of pie can catch up to it."

"Thank you, Louis."

I started up the stairs, balancing the plates.

"Don't forget, we're going to New York, New York tomorrow night." Gay Pride was ten days away and people were already beginning to celebrate. It was worse than Christmas.

When I got upstairs, I put the pie and beef into my nearly

empty refrigerator next to the chicken potpie and chocolate cake from Sunday's dinner.

My involvement in the death of Guy Peterson had been something of a wake-up call. I needed to take better care of myself. After all, I'd nearly ended up dead. When I asked myself how that happened, the only good answer I could come up with was that I was trying to be a nice—if somewhat nosey—person. But if my choice was between being a nice dead person or a horrible living person, then I'd rather be horrible. So my plan was to do everything I could to mind my own business.

Speaking of my business, things at my video store, Pinx Video, were looking up. Mikey Kellerman, my self-appointed number one employee, had convinced me to stock some personal lubricants under the counter to sell to people when they rented X-rated movies, and the lubes were selling well. I wouldn't be able to retire to the Riviera, but Pinx was making enough profit each month for me to get by. Barely.

The store was on Hyperion, wedged between a dry cleaner and a Mexican takeout place named Taco Maria. It had two enormous plate-glass windows that we kept filled with posters for recent and upcoming videos. Inside were several rows of shelves with video boxes and a counter for checking tapes in and out. Behind the counter was a storeroom where we kept the actual videos.

I walked in about a half an hour before we were set to open and found Mikey at work on a special project. Around thirty-five, he wore a pair of faded jeans, a pink T-shirt and Chuck Taylors. He kept his light brown hair closely shorn in hopes that the bald patch would be less noticeable.

He'd emptied four shelves in the new releases section, reducing it by a third, and had made a construction paper sign that said, HIDDEN TREASURES. He was planning to feature quality movies that our customers were consistently ignoring, which in my mind meant they were also likely to be black-and-white classics from the thirties, forties and fifties. In fact, what I'd said to him was that it would be easier to simply rename the classics section.

"You know, I didn't actually agree to this," I pointed out.

"It's going to work, I promise."

I just scowled at him.

He smiled and said, "The mail is on your desk."

I went back to my tiny office and went through the mail. Sitting behind my desk, I tossed a couple of flyers from real estate agents into the waste can, flipped through a J. Crew catalog—promising myself I'd never tie a sweater around my neck again—and then opened a letter from my insurance company.

My heart nearly stopped beating. They'd raised my health insurance from one hundred and fifty-six dollars to one thousand ninety-two dollars a month. It was not entirely a surprise. I'd heard this could happen after you went on AZT, which I'd done about seven weeks earlier. I'd considered buying the AZT on my own, but that seemed to defeat the whole purpose of health insurance. Of course, I hadn't known exactly how much they'd be increasing my rate. A nine hundred dollar jump might have changed my mind.

I wondered if it would be cheaper to go without insurance, but that seemed a bad idea as well. The cost of my medications was nearly five hundred dollars each month. And then there were the blood tests every two weeks, which cost as much as the medication—and might also have triggered a spike in my insurance. Add on the doctor visits and I'd probably be spending more than the insurance company wanted to charge me. But still, that extra nine hundred dollars wasn't in my budget.

The phone rang. It was still a few minutes before we opened, so I was fairly certain Mikey was still busily working on his HIDDEN TREASURES shelf. I picked up the phone.

"Pinx Video," I said.

"Noah, please," a woman's voice said. A voice I recognized.

"Judith?"

"Oh. It's you."

"What can I do for you?" I asked, stiffly. Our last conversation had not been pleasant.

"I wonder if you'd like to have lunch."

That was a stunning offer. Judith was my late partner—er, lover's sister. In a way, she had been my sister-in-law. When Jeffer died, for various reasons, my relationship with his family had swiftly deteriorated. And now, a year later, she wanted to go to lunch.

I left a long enough pause that she asked, "Noah, are you still there?"

"Yes, yes I am. Lunch?"

"I know it's the last thing you were expecting."

"It is."

"Why don't you pick the restaurant?" she suggested, as though that somehow made up for things.

"I haven't said I'll go," I pointed out.

"Look, I called you. Shouldn't that count for something?"

It should count for something, I just wasn't sure exactly what. Did it mean she was going to apologize? Were we going to let bygones be bygones and resume some sort of familial relationship? Or did she have something else in mind?

Since there was only one way to find out, I said, "La Casita Grande at one o'clock."

After the call, I went into the tiny employee bathroom and looked at myself in the mirror. My hair—which on a good day was thick and unruly—looked like a bramble bush. To be honest, I didn't know what a bramble bush looked like, but it sounded as terrible as my hair looked.

I tried not to look closely at myself. Louis was right; I had lost weight. Not that I had much to lose. The result was that my ears stuck out a tiny bit more than usual, which unfortunately made me look even more like an elf. It seemed very unfair. If I had to look like a mythical creature what was wrong with resembling a Greek god or even a vampire? I didn't really want to look like a prolific toymaker.

Of course, I was wearing the wrong outfit. I had on a pair of cream-colored corduroy pants, a celery-colored, vintage velour shirt I'd gotten at St. Vincent De Paul, and a pair of drugstore flip-flops. I was going to have to go home, re-shower, struggle with my hair, and choose an outfit that would shame and humiliate Judith, while pointing up the fact that I was a far better person than she. And I had only two hours to do it.

Mikey was thrilled that I was leaving. Really, I think he'd fire me if it weren't for the fact that I owned the place and was, at least symbolically, his boss. I rushed out of the store and was back home in less than ten minutes.

Fifteen minutes later I stood in front of the bathroom mirror, blow dryer and brush in hand, ready to take on my hair. I'd had it cut three weeks before and was definitely at the midpoint between haircuts. I basically had two choices: try to make all of my hair stand up or coax it into lying down. I did know that no matter how hard I tried to do either of those things my hair would do neither, choosing instead some combination of standing up and lying down. I did my best to make it all lie down and refused to look at it again.

I put on a pair of loose fitting black jeans, my Docs, a white T-shirt and, finally, a blue plaid flannel shirt worn like a jacket. It wasn't remotely cold out, but I knew the air conditioning at La Casita Grande could sometimes be arctic and I tended to chill easily.

Pulling my little red Sentra into the restaurant's parking lot at about ten after one, I was, what we call in L.A., on time. The restaurant had once been a small mansion. It had about six rooms on the first floor that had been opened up with cutouts and pass-throughs, giving the place a feeling of openness. Each room was painted in a different vibrant color and decorated with the kind of souvenirs that cost pennies in Tijuana. The hostess led me to a table for two in the lime green room, and there sat Judith Cole.

In her early forties, she was elegantly thin, wore her blond hair long and perfectly highlighted. She favored little black dresses, and that day her LBD was a sleeveless mini she wore with bare legs and strappy leather sandals. On the floor next to her sat a gigantic leather purse. She didn't wear any jewelry other than a gold wedding ring. When she saw me, she tossed her hair over her shoulder and crossed her legs. A margarita sat in front of her.

Not bothering with a 'hello' or 'how've you been,' I asked the question that had been bothering me since she called.

"Why now? What happened to change your mind?"

She flinched. "It's just, well, I think enough time has passed. It seems like the right thing to do."

A middle-aged waitress in a Mexican peasant dress came over and asked if I'd like anything to drink. I ordered an iced tea. Then she walked away.

Judith took a sip of her margarita and said, "I hope you've been well. I'm sure Tiffany would like to see you. I think you're her favorite uncle."

Judith's over-indulged child had always made it clear she couldn't stand me. "How old is she now?"

"Eight going on fourteen."

"That must be pleasant for you."

"You have no idea." She looked down at her drink. I realized she may not have actually looked at me since I sat down. "Look, the only excuse I can make for the way my family behaved is that we were angry. That happens, doesn't it? People get angry when someone dies and they take it out on each other?"

I appreciated that; it felt almost sincere.

"I'm sorry that we directed our anger at you," she said.

The waitress came back with my iced tea and took our order. Judith asked for a combination plate and a second margarita. I asked for a chicken taco—no salsa—and a side of rice.

When the waitress left, I grew nervous. I'd decided to do something before I left my apartment and nothing Judith said had changed my mind.

Here we go, I thought.

I took my pills out of my pocket, my hand shaking just a tiny bit. Unwrapping the tissue I'd carried them in, I carefully laid them out next to my plate: Bactrim, a simple white pill; AZT, a distinctive light blue and white capsule with a dark blue stripe down the center; and a third, tiny pink pill I'd started taking for nausea, Meda-Meca-something or other.

I was being a terrible drama queen, but I didn't care. Judith's eyes opened a little wider. She knew what AZT looked like. I was sure she'd given it to her brother. She stared at the pills for a long time. Then they began to embarrass me so I picked them up and swallowed them with a big gulp of water.

"I'm sorry. I didn't know," she said.

"Jeffer did. He knew."

"You found out before he died? I see."

"No. I mean he knew before we met. He knew he was positive before we met. He lied to me."

"That's not true. It can't be true."

She sipped her margarita and tried not to show any emotion. I had some idea what she was going through, trying to reconcile this fact with the brother she knew. Finding that there had been hints all along, things that should have told her something like this was possible, even likely. But, like all of us, like me, she'd ignored those hints. Given them a different spin. Convinced herself that her charming, thoughtful, decent brother couldn't also—

"I suppose that explains why he was always so nice about you. He wouldn't let us say a word against you."

"That's not the same as telling you the truth."

"No, it's not."

She seemed to regroup then, and got down to business. Her business. "Well, perhaps it's fortunate I called. I want to talk to you about Jeffer's memorabilia collection."

"What? What memorabilia collection?" I was surprised. I truly had no idea what she was talking about. "I mean, there's the blue chair you wouldn't let me have that was from the Sigourney Weaver movie he worked on. And there were a few other things like that, but I would never call that a collection."

"No, he had other things. Things from classic movies. Props and costumes."

I thought Jeffer Cole had lost the ability to shock me. But if this was true, if there was a memorabilia collection somewhere, it was shocking that he'd hidden it from me. Well, maybe it shouldn't be shocking, but it was.

Our lunches arrived. Neither of us lifted a fork.

"We'll give you ten thousand dollars for the collection."

"I'm not lying to you, Judith, I don't know anything about it."

"I'm sure you could use the money, given the situation."

Picking up my taco, I took a bite. I didn't want it. I wasn't even remotely hungry but if I didn't eat close to the time I took my medication I'd get sick even with the nausea medication. It also gave me a few moments to think things through.

When Jeffer died, Judith, her older brother, Jasper, and her parents had hired a lawyer and threatened to contest the will. He'd left everything to me, and in order to do that had outlined our loving relationship, which was as close as we could legally come to a marriage. The fact that I'd left Jeffer—though I did continue to see him—threatened the foundation of the will, so we'd negotiated, effectively splitting up what really should have been my assets.

The thing I realized as I swallowed my taco was, had Judith known about this collection of memorabilia at the time it would have been part of the negotiation. And that meant Jeffer never told her about it. Which begged the question, "How did you find out about the collection?"

"Jeffer told me, right before he died."

"No, he didn't. You're lying."

"I didn't come here to be insulted. I came to make you an offer. A very fair offer, I think."

"If you'd known about the collection before Jeffer died you wouldn't have waited more than a year to try and get your hands on it. You would have had your lawyer try to get a piece of it when you got everything else."

"You're making me sound positively mercenary." She picked up her fork and pushed her refried beans around the plate.

"Have you considered the possibility that whoever told you about the collection was lying?"

"Yes, but why would they—" She stopped, her cheeks

flushing as she realized she'd given herself away. That she'd just admitted someone other than Jeffer had told her about the collection.

"I'm not going to sit here and be disrespected," she said, as though I had been the one lying. She stood up, took her wallet out of the giant leather purse, and tossed a couple of twenties onto the table. "If you change your mind, the offer still stands."

Then, she stormed out of La Casita Grande. As I forced myself to eat a few more bites of my taco, I realized that I could make ten thousand dollars if I just found Jeffer's collection.

The money would come in handy. It would pay for nearly a year of insurance. If the collection actually existed, that is.

2

"Can we roll a few of the windows down?" I asked. We were in Marc's Infiniti on the way to New York, New York for happy hour. An Indigo Girls cassette was playing. They were getting closer to fine, whatever that meant. It was probably a lesbian thing. There were four of us in the car: Marc and Louis, Leon, and myself. We'd each worn a different cologne and the mix was making me dizzy.

"Are you all right?" Louis asked.

"It's just—the combination of the different colognes is starting to bother me."

Marc powered down all the windows. The sounds and smells of L.A. on a summer night drifted in, and I was reminded why people drive around with the windows up and the air conditioning on full blast. Still, they were easier on me than the blend of lemony, oaky, woodsy, masculinity.

"Perhaps in the future we should coordinate and all wear the same one," Leon suggested. "We could be the Aramis gang."

"I think I just need to avoid close spaces," I said, noticing that Marc had turned onto Sunset Boulevard and was heading in the wrong direction. "Where are we going?"

"We're taking a little detour."

We veered onto Santa Monica and continued west. I had an

inkling where we were going and I wasn't sure how I felt about it. My lunch with Judith had left me with a lot of gnawing questions and a sick feeling in my stomach that was definitely not an AZT side effect.

The Indigo Girls ended and Louis dug through a shoebox to find another cassette. He put on Whitney Houston, who really wanted to dance with someone. Why? Why couldn't she just dance alone?

"Did you see? Peter Allen died yesterday," Leon said.

"Liza Minnelli's gay husband?" Louis asked.

"I think he accomplished a few other things," Leon said. "But yes, Liza Minnelli's gay husband."

"That's sad," Marc said.

"AIDS."

"Sad and depressing."

I just looked out the window, ignoring the conversation. When we got to Mariposa and Santa Monica, Marc turned onto Mariposa and parked. Across the street was a three-story tall warehouse. There was a door at the back that had a small neon sign above it saying, Mercy Costumes. We all stared at the building.

"Do you think anyone's working on a Friday night?" Marc asked.

"This is the costume house where the costumer was killed," I guessed.

"It is," said Louis.

"Tell me what happened," I said. My stomach was definitely unsettled.

"Well," Leon began. "They say he was killed during a robbery. Shot. Except, no one can figure out what was taken."

"It was Anthony Mercer, wasn't it?"

"Oh my God, how did you know that?" Leon asked.

"It's Mercy Costumes. I knew him," I said, and that was what had been giving me a stomachache.

"You *did*?"

"Leon, close your mouth," Louis said. "If you were wearing dentures they'd have fallen out by now."

"Anthony was a friend of Jeffer's. He came to dinner once. He and Jeffer worked together at Lorimar for a while."

"Your boyfriend was a costumer?" Leon asked.

I shook my head. "Production designer. He did a little bit of everything. And he worked with everyone."

"Well, isn't it a small world."

"It is a small world," I said. "There are only eight costume houses in the city and two of them are owned by studios. If you work in the business you know everyone else who works in the business." I couldn't count the number of times Jeffer had bemoaned this simple fact.

"So are you going to help us figure this out?" Marc asked.

"I don't think I have a choice."

"Because you knew Anthony?" Leon wondered.

"It gets weirder than that."

And then I told them about my lunch with Judith.

"That's creepy," said Marc. "Who is she to show up out of nowhere demanding your stuff."

"Stuff I don't have."

"Even if you don't have it, it's still yours."

"Now, wait a minute," said Louis. "Anthony Mercer was killed over something he either didn't have or no one knew he had, since they can't figure out what was stolen. And now you've been offered ten thousand dollars for things you don't have, or don't know you have. This is all very peculiar."

"Yes, it is," I agreed.

"Let's see if there's anyone in there," Marc said, hitting the button that rolled up all the windows. We got out of the car, and he immediately lit a cigarette, taking several quick drags while we crossed the street.

The door, of course, was locked. There was a bell next to it, so Leon rang it. We waited a while, long enough for Marc to finish his cigarette. Above the door a security camera stared down at us. The boys noticed where I was looking so they all looked up, too. That's when the door finally opened a crack and a very petite, very pale woman in her early twenties looked out at us.

"Yes?"

"We were friends with Anthony. We're wondering if we could talk to someone about him," Marc said.

"You don't look like friends of Anthony."

Anthony was black, and it seemed she thought all of his friends should be too.

"We were more like acquaintances," I said. "My lover, Jeffer Cole, worked with him years ago."

"Oh, yeah. Anthony talked about Jeffer."

"Could we come in?" I asked.

"All right."

She stepped back to let us in. For a tiny girl, she wore a lot of clothing: two filmy floral skirts of different lengths, black cowboy boots, a peasant top with a bolero jacket over it, two-dozen thin rubber bracelets on one wrist, and a tomato-shaped pincushion on the other. Atop her head she wore an old, floppy fedora with a plastic daisy stuck into the band.

Inside, the warehouse was dark, cool and smelled like a dusty attic. It was also bulging at the seams with clothes. Rolling wardrobe racks surrounded us as soon as we entered. There were also clothes above us hung on the kind of motorized track system you'd find at a dry cleaner, though on a much grander scale. The track hung above us and circled the circumference of the building, at least twice. Hanging from it were hundreds and hundreds of clothing items.

In the center of it all was a large worktable with stools placed around it, a collection of dress forms in various sizes standing guard nearby, and several open shelves crammed full of bolts of fabric. There was a small desk with an aging computer sitting on it, and a wall phone attached to a post.

The five of us gathered uncomfortably around the work-table. The table was about six feet by ten feet. On the side opposite where Willow sat, *Jeopardy!* played on a nine-inch portable TV.

"Are you here all alone, Miss…?" Louis asked.

"Willow," she said. "Willow Epstein. And, no, I'm not alone. Kerry's here somewhere."

It wasn't that hard to see how you might mislay a person in a place like that. Willow sat on a stool and picked up a gold lamé blouse she was repairing.

"So, how is Jeffer? Does he need an assistant?"

"He passed away last year."

She frowned as though it was a personal inconvenience. "Bummer."

"I'm sorry about what happened to Anthony," I said.

"We all are," Leon added.

"Oh my God, it's been awful," Willow said, stating the obvious. "Anthony was the best boss I ever had."

"I work at Paramount," Leon said. "A lot of rumors are going around. It's all people can talk about."

"Yeah. We do a lot of your shows."

"Was Anthony here alone when it happened?" I asked.

"Well, no," Willow said, as though the question was foolish. "It wasn't suicide. He was with whoever killed him."

"Right, of course. But there was no one else in the building? Other than the two of them?"

"I don't know. I wasn't here. He sent me home early. He sent us all home early."

"Why did he—?"

"People are saying it was a robbery gone wrong," Leon said.

I wanted to know why he sent his people home early and didn't appreciate being interrupted like that. I gave Leon a look.

Willow took the opportunity to ask, "So, like, what are you guys? Gay Charlie's Angels?"

"No, we're just far too nosey for our own good," Louis said.

"Oh, well, that wouldn't bother Anthony. He was all about other people's business."

"He liked to gossip?"

"He lived for it. He knew everything about everyone. The producers of *Tonight's Entertainment News* called at least once a week."

"He gave them sto—" I started to ask.

"You don't keep a lot of money around, do you?" Leon

again. This time I didn't just give him a look, I gave him a dirty look. He didn't need to keep interrupting me.

"No. We don't have money around. We invoice the studios and then actually getting paid is like pulling teeth. The only time of the year we ever have money around is Halloween. That's when we're open to the public. We rent costumes for the holiday."

"Did you notice anything odd about Anthony on the day he died? Was he unhappy or distracted?" Marc asked.

"No. Actually, he was happy. He was supposed to have a date."

"Really? Do you know who it was with?"

"No. It was a blind date."

"From the personal ads or did a friend set him up?" Marc kept on her.

"I think the personals. He was always carrying around last week's *Frontiers*." There were personal ads in the back that you could answer by calling a voicemail system.

"Was that why he sent everyone home early?" I asked.

"Oh yeah, it was."

"So it's possible his date was here when he was killed?"

"I guess," she admitted.

I looked at Marc and Louis and said, "Maybe it wasn't a robbery gone wrong; maybe it was a romance gone wrong."

"Very wrong," Louis remarked.

"Well…" Willow said.

"What is it?" I asked.

"Things were all messed up. That's why the police think it was a robbery. The whole place was a mess. It took Kerry and me all week to get it sorted out."

"Is there an office?" I asked.

"Not really, Anthony liked to spend his time right here at the worktable. That's why the phone has such a long cord." I glanced over at the wall phone and noted that it did indeed have a very long cord. And that reminded me of something. "You said the producers of *Tonight's Entertainment News* called him every week. Did he sell them stories?"

"He said he didn't," she said, nervously. It was a touchy subject. If he'd gotten caught selling stories he would have lost clients. A lot of clients.

"Why did they call every week if—"

"Do you know if anything is missing?" Leon interrupted me again. I almost kicked him in the shins but thought better of it.

She shrugged. "Not everything is catalogued. We have a temp come in twice a week trying to catch us up. But we're only through half of what we have."

"What do you mean when you say catalogued?" Louis asked, though of the four of us my guess was he already had the best idea.

"Each garment has a number. Then it gets a brief description, it's assigned a period, an overall color, a gender."

"So you can make a list of all the Victorian men's suits you have?" Leon asked.

"Eventually, yes."

I hated having to ask this, "Where did it happen? Where was Anthony killed?"

"Right here."

"Right here, where?"

"Where you're standing."

I moved.

"We cleaned it up. It was really gross."

We were quiet and uncomfortable for a few moments. Finally, Leon asked, "Is the business going to continue?"

"Sort of. Billy Martinez is already talking about buying us."

"Who's Billy Martinez?" Marc asked.

"The owner of Hollywood Costume," I said.

"I really hope that doesn't happen," Willow said.

"Why not?"

"Anthony hated Billy Martinez. He'd be really upset if…if he knew."

———

New York, New York was even more crowded than usual. In

preparation for the upcoming Gay Pride, they'd decorated the narrow, Big Apple-themed bar with balloons in rainbow colors and a gigantic rainbow flag tacked up on the ceiling.

They never bothered with a DJ, so the music tended toward the top one hundred pop tunes the jukebox provided. Mariah Carey was singing "I'll Be There" when we walked in. Louis volunteered to fight his way to the bar, while the rest of us stubbornly tried to stake a claim to about four square feet of floor space.

"That was cute that she thought we were the gay Charlie's Angels," Marc said.

"The only thing I remember about that show was that there was the smart one. There was the pretty one. And there was the one that was Farrah Fawcett," Leon said.

"Generally speaking, why would you kill a costumer?" Marc asked.

"To steal his business," I suggested. "Billy Martinez wants to take over. He'd practically have a monopoly if he could get his hands on Mercy Costumes."

"You think this Martinez person had him killed so they could buy his business?" Marc asked.

"I don't know. You said 'generally speaking.' It is a good reason to kill a costume designer, don't you think?"

A cocktail waiter selling rainbow Jell-O shots came by. They were missing half the colors, but they were still cute and very effective. Leon bought four. There was no sign of Louis.

"What else?" Marc asked. "What are the other possibilities?"

Leon handed out the Jell-O shots, then ran his tongue around the paper cup his shot came in and sucked up the Jell-O pellet. When he swallowed he said, "International drug cartel?"

"And how would that work?" I asked.

"Sew the drugs into the lining of costumes," Leon suggested.

"You've seen too many Bruce Willis movies."

"How many is too many?"

"One." Marc and I said at once.

I stared at my Jell-O shot. I was supposed to avoid alcohol, it didn't mix well with my meds. But I was sure this was mostly Jell-O. I squeezed the paper cup into my mouth. It was sweet, and stronger than I'd hoped.

"Then there's *Tonight's Entertainment Network*," I said after I swallowed. "If Billy was selling them stories he might have crossed the wrong person."

By the time Louis got there with a tray of drinks we'd heard "Finally," something by Abba, and one by George Michael, who just wanted our sex. It was still two-for-one happy hour, so Marc and Louis each had a Ketel One and soda, while Leon juggled two Ketel One and cranberry juices. I had a bottle of Calistoga with a lime, which apparently was not two for one.

Louis asked, "What did I miss?"

"Nothing really," I said.

"We were just thinking up logical motives for killing a costumer," Marc explained.

There was a lull and I took advantage of it. I turned to Leon and said, "Did you have to keep interrupting me?"

"I have no idea what you're talking about. Besides, you didn't even want to be there."

"Well, I was there, and you kept interrupting me."

"Children," Louis said. "Am I going to have to turn this car around?"

Leon pursed his lips and said, "Sorry."

Now I felt stupid for bringing it up. But really glad I didn't kick him in the shins. "Don't worry about it."

"What about jealousy?" Marc suggested. "Maybe he stole a client from another designer and they just wouldn't have it."

"That's a fun theory," Louis said. "But doesn't it need to have something to do with Noah's sister-in-law showing up out of nowhere? Remember, she wants something that she thinks Noah has. And whoever killed Anthony wanted something they thought he had. So do they want the same thing?"

"Yes."

"Probably."

"Maybe."

"Okay," Louis said. "What is it?"

"I want to say a costume," I said. "But it just seems ridiculous to kill someone over a costume."

"Your sister-in—"

"Judith," I said. I didn't really want to call her my sister-in-law. She wasn't legally and she certainly wasn't in any other way, shape or form.

"Judith used the word memorabilia, right?" Louis asked.

"Yes, she did."

"So it's some old movie costume."

"Or a prop. Jeffer worked more with those actually."

"But you wouldn't go to a costume shop to steal a prop."

"No, you wouldn't."

"Well, that does seem ridiculous. I agree with Noah. It's hard to believe someone being killed over some old costume," Marc said.

"Not if the costume is really famous. I would kill for one of Scarlett O'Hara's dresses," Leon said.

"Or something Marilyn Monroe wore," Louis added.

"But I can't imagine that Jeffer had anything like that."

"So, what should we do next?" Leon asked.

"I should call Detective O'Shea," I said. Detective Javier O'Shea was a homicide detective who worked out of the Rampart Division. We'd met just a few weeks before when I—well we actually—stuck our noses into the Guy Peterson murder. It was very possible this murder was his, too.

The idea of calling him didn't make anyone happy.

"I suppose that's the right thing to do," Louis said.

"It's just that he's going to want us to butt out," Marc said.

"Well, we just won't let him spoil our fun," Leon said, "will we?"

The conversation drifted to our plans for the weekend. Marc and Louis were going to a couple of open houses. They were nowhere near ready to buy a house but loved looking. Leon had a date that he'd pulled out of the back of *Frontiers*.

"As soon as I read his ad, VGL GHM ISO GWM HWP for LTR…well, he had me at LTR."

"I didn't understand any of that," I said.

"Because you don't date. If you're going to date you have to learn a whole new language."

"So how does it work? You read his ad and wrote him a letter?"

"Oh my God, you really haven't been dating," Leon crowed, though I had no idea why it seemed to amuse him. "No, he has a voice mailbox. You call the general number and input the number at the end of an ad, and then you say hello and whatever else and leave your phone number."

"So he called you?"

"He has the most charming accent."

"I don't know why you go to the trouble," Louis said. "You could just hang out at the Mercado."

I broke down and had a Ketel One and cranberry. Leon wandered off to flirt with a really cute Latino guy. The crowd thinned a tiny bit. I bought another drink, but began to feel nauseated halfway through. Ten minutes later I was in the bathroom throwing up. Take my word for it, there is nothing in life as disgusting as vomiting in a crowded gay bar. Nothing.

Marc and Louis insisted on taking me home—they were ready to change bars anyway and were happy to stop at home on their way to the Gauntlet. Leon had disappeared entirely, though the boys didn't seem particularly concerned about abandoning him.

A half an hour after getting sick I was feeling better. I grabbed a red-and-black afghan my mother had knitted me, curled up in my POONG easy chair from IKEA, and was watching *Valley of the Dolls*—for the fifth time—while nibbling on saltines and sipping flat ginger ale.

3

———

THE NEXT MORNING, AFTER A FEW HOURS SLEEP, I FELT better and, making a mental list of everything I needed to do, hurried down the thirty-six rusty red steps down to my garage. Blocking it was a long, flat limousine. It was at least twenty-some years old and black with black-tinted windows. The back window hummed as it rolled down. Then, surprisingly, Wilma Wanderly leaned out and asked, "Young man, are you Noah Valentine?"

I was stunned. The movie star, Wilma Wanderly was talking to me. And she knew my name. How did that happen?

"Um, yes, I'm Noah."

"Wonderful. Get in. I need to talk to you."

The passenger door opened opposite to the way car doors normally opened and I climbed in. Now, I did know better than to get into vehicles with people I didn't know. But it was Wilma Wanderly, so in a way I *did* know her. I'd grown up on her movies.

In the dark of the limousine, I realized she was in full makeup first thing in the morning and the blond helmet of hair on her head was likely an elaborate wig. She probably thought she looked about fifty, but really she looked exactly like what she was—a seventy-year-old woman trying too hard to look fifty.

"How did you know where I live?"

"You're in the phone book," a man said, startling me. I hadn't noticed him there. In the inky night of the limo I could barely make him out. From what I could see, he was homely and somewhere between thirty and fifty.

"My assistant, Albert," Wilma said. "Albert, give him one of my cards."

Albert reached into his shirt pocket, pulled out a silver business card holder, and promptly dropped it onto the floor of the limo.

"Oh for God's sake," Wilma said.

Albert was down on the floor feeling around for the business cards in the dark. I couldn't be sure, but I think she may have kicked him. "Here it is," he said, as he got back onto his seat, opened the holder, and took out a card for me. Then he handed it to me. I glanced at it; it was a bright white card printed with royal blue ink. I put it into my pocket.

"Do you have one?" she asked.

I didn't. "Um, you already know where I live."

"That's right, I do!" she laughed. "Now, let's get down to business. Do you have my dress?"

It was a strange question. Though after the possibilities I'd discussed with the boys the night before, perhaps not that strange. I said, "No. I don't have your dress," because I didn't.

She tried again. "I've been told your deceased lover had my dress from *The Girl From Albany*. I'd like you to give it to me."

"But I don't have it." Although, I now assumed it was part of the imaginary collection of memorabilia Judith was looking for.

"Did you give it to someone else?" she asked.

"No. I mean, I never had it. So I couldn't give it to someone else."

"It's blue. Sequined." Albert said, in case I had dozens of Wilma Wanderly's old dresses and simply couldn't figure out which one we were talking about.

"I know what the dress looks like." Then to Wilma I said, "I've seen most of your movies."

"Most?"

"Well, the ones on VHS, I mean."

"Oh but you haven't lived until you've seen me on the big screen. They show them all the time at that art house on the Westside…"

She snapped her fingers until Albert supplied, "The Nuart Theatre."

"Yes, that's the one. Don't deny yourself. Go."

"Yes, ma'am."

She sighed and then, as though remembering why we were there, said, "I'll give you twenty-five thousand dollars for the dress."

"I'm sorry, I can't sell you something I don't have. Not at any price."

"Mother, he doesn't have it."

"I've told you not to call me mother when there are people around."

"Yes, Miss Wanderly."

I sighed. She simply wasn't going to believe I didn't have the dress. "Look, I had lunch with Jeffer's sister yesterday and she seemed—"

"Judith," Wilma supplied.

Things began to come together. "Oh, I see. You offered Judith twenty-five thousand for the dress, didn't you?"

"Don't be silly. I only offered her twenty. I offered you more because I'm getting desperate."

"Mo—Miss Wanderly, don't tell people you're desperate. It's not a good negotiating tactic."

"But I *am* desperate. I should be allowed to say it."

"Are you the one who told Judith about Jeffer's memorabilia collection?"

"She claimed to know nothing about it. Obviously, she was lying."

"Who told you Jeffer had your dress?"

"That's neither here nor there.

"I'd say it's very here or there," I said, realizing how dumb that sounded coming out of my mouth. "Look, you really should tell me who told you. It might help me figure out what happened to the dress."

She turned away from me and held a hand in front of her face.

"Miss Wanderly is tired," Albert said. He held out a business card saying, "Please call us if you find you have the dress."

"You already gave me a card," I pointed out.

"Oh, sorry. I think you should go."

Clumsily, I felt around until I found the door handle and then got out of the car. Shutting the door behind me, I stepped back and stared. That had to be one of the most bizarre conversations of my life.

Before the limo pulled away, the rear window hummed down again, and Wilma Wanderly leaned her head out and said, "Be careful, Mr. Valentine. I'm not the only one who wants the dress."

When she said it, it sounded exactly like something out of an old movie.

Of course, I should have asked her if she knew anything about Anthony Mercer's death. Not that she would have told me if she did, but I would have liked to have seen her reaction. After the limo pulled away, I opened the metal gate to my garage/carport, got into my little red Sentra, and pulled it out into the street. Leaving it running, I got out and closed the gate again.

Then I did exactly what I'd planned to do before I'd been interrupted: I drove to Rampart Station. I was able to park across the street and then cross Temple at the crosswalk. The steps leading into Rampart were right there at the corner. As I started up them, I glanced at a really good-looking guy coming down them. He was tall, with dark hair, a square jaw and light brown eyes. I was too busy cruising him to realize—

"Noah? Noah Valentine?" he asked.

Shit. It was Detective Javier O'Shea and I hadn't even realized it. It had been a few months, but that was no excuse. He wore a light gray linen suit with a barely gray shirt underneath. His tie was black silk with a chalk stripe. Honestly, I think *Miami Vice* was the worst thing ever to happen to cops; now they all thought they had to be fashion plates.

"Um, hi. I came to see you," I said.

"Is it important? I'm on my way to court."

"Um, it'll only take a minute."

"Okay, shoot."

Then, instead of telling him why I was there, I stupidly asked, "You don't have a partner?"

"They do that on television so that the characters have someone to talk to. Real police work is a guy driving around by himself. Not too dramatic. Even when we do work partners, it's usually just two guys in a car not talking."

"Uh-huh."

I'd noticed he was good-looking during the whole Guy Peterson fiasco, but I didn't remember him being this—

"You didn't come down here to ask if I had a partner, did you?"

"Oh, um, no. Is the Mercer murder yours?"

"I'm on that case, yes. Why? Was he a friend of yours?"

"Not a friend, exactly."

"What exactly then?"

"My late boyfriend—" Oh, that sounded so odd, as though my boyfriend was late and would be arriving at any moment. "I was with Jeffer Cole for five years, almost six. He was a production designer. He's the one who knew Anthony. We had him to our house a few times for dinner."

"So far this isn't very helpful."

"Jeffer's sister contacted me yesterday. She wanted to buy Jeffer's collection of Hollywood memorabilia from me."

"And why is that important?"

"I don't have it. I'd never even heard of it."

"I really do have someplace to be."

"You're not seeing this. Anthony was killed for something, but we don't know what. Judith wants something from me, but I don't know what."

"So, your big tip is that you don't know."

"Except, I do know. I think this is all about a blue sequined dress. I met Wilma Wanderly this morning."

"The old-time actress?"

"Yes. She wore the dress in one of her movies and now she wants it back."

"Enough to kill?"

"Maybe. Or maybe the killing part was a mistake."

"Anthony Mercer was shot execution-style. He was made to get on his knees and then shot in the back of the head. There's no mistake about it. It was very professional."

Suddenly, I felt like everything I'd been thinking was wrong. Something else was going on and it had nothing to do with a dress. Anthony must have been in debt to organized crime or was involved with a gang somehow. How could being killed execution-style have anything to do with a blue sequined dress from the 1940s?

"Maybe I've made a mistake," I said.

"What's the sister's name?"

"Judith. Judith Cole."

"All right. You've told me what I needed to know. Now I want you to go home and stay out of this. Do you understand me?"

"I do understand you. It's just that people keep showing up."

He narrowed his gorgeous eyes at me and said, "Tell them to go away."

After I left Rampart, I drove directly to Pinx Video. Breezing in, I said hello to Mikey and then went to my office in the back. I spent a good three hours working on the 1991 taxes for the store. I had four more months to pull everything together and give it to my accountant, and I was going to need it. Then I'd have to start on 1992.

It was close to three o'clock and I knew I had to eat something. I was late taking my pills, so I went down to Taco Maria and ordered their chicken enchiladas and a giant root beer to go. Walking back into Pinx, I saw that Missy had arrived. She'd dressed for the occasion, wearing red Doc Marten boots, black tights, a pleated Catholic schoolgirl skirt, a black motorcycle jacket and a T-shirt that said Nirvana. Her hair was curly and copious, and had probably needed a half a bottle of mousse to look that carefree.

Mikey and Missy barely got along. That made Thursday, Friday and Saturday, the days their shifts overlapped, the most uncomfortable of the week. It also made them the days I most needed to be there.

There were several people in line checking out videos. Mikey and Missy were both working behind the counter. I stopped at the Hidden Treasures display, looking through it until I found what I wanted: *The Girl From Albany*. I stepped over to the counter, slipped into the storeroom behind it, and pulled the tape. As I came back out, I heard Missy ask the customer she was waiting on, "Would you like lube with that?"

The guy mumbled something sounding like "No thanks" and then slunk out of the store. I stood behind her and asked, "What did you just do?"

"What do you mean?"

Mikey was finishing up a sale, so as quietly as possible I said, "Don't ask the customers if they'd like lube with their pornos."

"That's what Mikey told me to do," Missy explained. She was smirking just a little and that gave me the feeling this had been a bone of contention between them.

Mikey finished his customer and turned to us to say, "It's called upselling. It's how McDonalds makes a kazillion dollars a year. No one buys a hamburger without being asked if they want fries with it."

"Personal lubricant and French fries are not the same thing."

"I told you he wouldn't like it," Missy said, unhelpfully.

"You have a problem with sex, don't you?" Mikey asked.

"I do not. And even if I did, this is not about me. It's about our customers. A lot of whom do have a problem with sex."

"Not the ones renting pornos."

"The ones next to the people renting pornos might—especially if they're with their kids."

"Noah, how do you expect to sell any lube if people don't know we have it?"

"You've got a display," I said, waving at the small display of personal lubricant next to the TV and VCR where we tested videos people complained about and showed movies people weren't renting.

"Nobody can see that."

"We can't have a display *and* ask every single person if they want lube."

"Fine, we'll get rid of the display."

"Keep the display. No more upselling."

And with that, I stormed off to my office with my lunch and video in hand.

The little office barely had room for a desk and a guest chair. Still, I'd managed to shove a 19" portable TV and a VCR player into the corner. Both sat atop a folding snack table. I had to sit backward in the guest chair in order to turn everything on and put the video into the VCR.

During the FBI Warning and the previews, I laid out my lunch and got my pills out. I'd been taking the pills for almost two months. I should probably get something to carry them around in other than a tissue, but plastic pillboxes seemed geriatric.

After taking a bite of the enchilada, I picked up the remote and fast-forwarded through almost the entire movie. I'd seen it before. Basically, *The Girl From Albany* is about a wide-eyed, wannabe actress (Wilma Wanderly) from New York State's capitol city who makes her way to Broadway, and through a series of comedic missteps winds up starring in a hit musical.

The movie climaxes with the lavish musical number "I'm Too Blue to Be Blue" in which she and the older, more experienced Dorothy Caine sing and dance up a storm.

The film was not considered very good—really not the hidden treasure Mikey was making it out to be—but the final number, which felt strangely disconnected from the rest of the film, was legendary. Wilma Wanderly and Dorothy Caine were both popular with female impersonators, and that alone meant that *The Girl From Albany* was a frequent rental at Pinx.

Once I'd cued up the scene, I swallowed all my pills, then hit play. The camera caught the two women on a wide, cream-colored stage that was probably larger than Times Square, though it was supposed to be inside a typical Broadway theater. They stood on a floating set of stairs that went nowhere; their shimmering cobalt dresses the focal point. The dresses were simple enough. They were each full length with plunging neck-lines and hip-high slits in the skirt. Each was carefully cut to the actress's body and then covered in light-catching blue sequins. Both women wore large hats made of white and blue ostrich features, as they sang, "I'm Too Blue to Be Blue."

"Once in a while, I cry 'til I smile," crooned Dorothy.

"And then I get mad, that I can't be sad," added Wilma.

Together they sang, "I'm too blue to be blue."

After that they picked up their four-foot long sequined trains and danced down the steps. Immediately, twelve tuxedoed dancers rushed in, six for each actress. The dancers deftly lifted Dorothy and Wilma up and floated them to opposite ends of the stage. The camera cut to a long shot as they women were set down. When you looked closely, their trains were perfectly arranged, so their landings must have ended up on the editing room floor.

What you didn't realize, largely because of the editing, was that Dorothy Caine was nearly a foot taller than Wilma Wanderly. When they stood next to each other they were shot close up and looked close to the same height—presumably because Wilma was standing on a box. It was only in the very few distance shots, in which they stood next to each other, that you could see how much bigger Dorothy was than Wilma.

"You broke my heart, and right from the start," warbled Dorothy.

"I've been so glad, that you're such a cad," answered Wilma.

"I'm too blue to be blue."

The twelve male dancers had lined up and, as they sang the chorus, each actress knocked over six dancers, one after the other. The dancers scrambled to their feet and formed a kick line—

My phone rang.

I picked it up. "Pinx Video."

"Noah, is that you?" my mother asked.

Just then Mikey picked up, "Pinx Video."

"Mikey, I've got this. It's my mother."

"Oh, sorry." He hung up.

"I don't mean to bother you at work, but I hadn't heard from you and I have to meet Carolyn Harvey. We're going to the senior showing of *Housesitter* and then we're having the early bird special at Bennigan's."

"That sounds fun. Have a good time."

"You're going to want to get a bunch of copies of *Housesitter*."

"Mom, you haven't seen it yet."

"Oh, I know, but it's going to be so good. Steve Martin and Goldie Hawn! If they can't make you laugh, you don't have a funny bone. Anyway, I could have waited until tomorrow, but Carolyn invited me to her church and I decided to go. I didn't want you calling and worrying about my not being here."

"I don't worry about you, Mom, you're doing great."

"You don't know, dear. Getting old is not for the faint of heart." She stopped for a moment and then said, "Oh my gosh, I shouldn't say that, should I? Jeffer didn't get to be very old, and it's not that he gave up, it's just—"

"It's all right. I understand what you meant. Getting old is hard." Actually, these days being young was sometimes hard too, but I decided not to say so. She'd want to know why I felt that way.

"Well, how are you?" she asked, as though I'd been doing my best not to tell her.

"I'm fine."

I was dying to tell her I'd met Wilma Wanderly, but I worried about what she'd think of Jeffer keeping secrets from me. It wasn't that I really cared whether she still liked him; it was that it mattered to her that she still liked him. If I was more honest about who Jeffer was, well, it felt like I'd be taking something away from her.

And then, after thinking all that, I told her anyway. "I met Wilma Wanderly."

She gasped. "You did? Did she come into the video store?"

That was the perfect lie. She'd just handed it to me. I could easily have said Miss Wanderly came in to rent a video, but I didn't.

"Not exactly. An old friend of Jeffer's passed away and she wanted to say how sorry she was." It was closer to the truth, but still a big fat lie.

"Oh, that was so nice of her. I always thought she'd be nice in person. Such a hard life, though, poor thing. Do you know she began performing when she was practically an infant? She said her first word on stage."

I had the feeling that was studio publicity, but my mother liked believing it so I let her.

"How did she look?"

"She looked wonderful. Every inch the movie star."

"Did you get her autograph?"

"No, there wasn't a convenient moment for that."

"When you see movie stars you really need to get their autographs. You could put them in the window of your store. It would draw more people."

It probably wouldn't in L.A., but I said, "Good idea. Well, I should get going. I am at work, after all."

"Oh, of course, I'll call you next weekend. Bye, bye."

After I hung up the phone, I tried to focus. Did Jeffer have the dress from *The Girl From Albany*? Did he have a secret collection of memorabilia? And if he did, who would know about it?

I came up with only one name.

4

ROBERT LIVED IN A WORLD WAR II ERA BUILDING IN WEST Hollywood, right below Sunset Boulevard. It wasn't actually *a* building; it was five. Five Spanish-style bungalows with two one-bedroom apartments in each bungalow. They looked like five tiny, stucco houses arranged in a U-shape around a simple courtyard. There was a sidewalk down the center, a couple of very tall, very old trees at the front, with various pots of plants and the occasional straight-backed chair set out by tenants to personalize their front stoops.

I met Robert, along with his best friend and next-door neighbor, Tina, when I worked as a waiter at Renaldo's—an Italian restaurant on the top floor of a twelve-story building in Hollywood a block or two from the Cinerama Dome. A few years older than me, Robert was tall and frequently sunburned, and had a tiny bit of curly blond hair that barely covered his head. He was the bartender at Renaldo's, and when I found out he had a theater degree with a focus in costuming I immediately connected him with Jeffer. He and Tina adored Jeffer and for a long time the four of us were thick as thieves. Then Jeffer got ill.

When he opened his front door, I said, "What do you know about the blue dress from *The Girl From Albany*?"

"I was half expecting you. I suppose you should come in."

Though Robert had lived in his apartment for years, it wasn't what you'd call decorated. There was a sofa—that I'd slept on for a few months after I left Jeffer—and a dining table with four chairs, and not much else. He'd worked for a couple of years with Jeffer on various projects and then took a job at Hollywood Costume for stability. I'd always felt like Robert used up all his creativity on his career and there wasn't anything left by the time he got home in the evening.

I sat down on the sofa, which was cheap and scratchy, while Robert sat in a chrome-and-black leather chair from the thirties that Jeffer had restored for my twenty-sixth birthday. Robert adored it, really more than I did, so I'd given it to him during the divorce, separation, whatever it was—the end is the phrase that feels best.

"Wilma Wanderly got in touch with you?" Robert asked.

"She showed up in front of my apartment in a big black limousine. Do I have you to thank for that?"

"All I know is that Wilma's looking for the dress. But everyone knows that. She's been looking for months."

I stared at him for a moment, not sure whether I should believe him. "Tell me about the dress. Tell me everything."

He sighed.

"Well, first of all, it's not one dress. It's two. Or rather, four. Whenever you film a scene like that you make backups. There were two dresses for Wilma and two for Dorothy Caine. That way if anything went wrong they could be filming again in just a few minutes."

"Okay, so what happened to the dresses?"

"After the movie wrapped Wilma and Dorothy were each given one of the dresses."

"Wilma didn't mention that."

"Well, no, she probably wouldn't. During the sixties and seventies she wore the dress in her Vegas act. In fact, she wore it out. Eventually it was nothing but shreds and was thrown away."

"What about Dorothy's dress?"

"That's a little murkier. Somehow, Wilma recently came into possession of Dorothy's dress. I'm not sure how."

"So if she's got one of the dresses what's the big deal?"

"They're most valuable as a set."

"So she wants the backup for her dress?"

"Yes, exactly."

"Why does she think Jeffer had it?"

"Maybe Judith told her."

"No, Judith didn't know about it until Wilma told her."

"Really? Well, that does surprise me. I knew it was a secret, but that doesn't mean people don't know."

"Jeffer *did* have it?"

"Yes, of course," Robert said simply. "Anthony Mercer and Dick Congdon found the backup dresses in a dumpster. They were being thrown away."

"I don't believe it."

"No, it's true. It was the late seventies. Things weren't going well at Warner Brothers. The lot wasn't even called Warner Brothers anymore. It was The Burbank Studios then, and they were sharing with Columbia. Can you imagine? Studio roommates. Anyway, there probably wasn't a lot of space for old costumes from the nineteen forties."

"So Dick Congdon gave Jeffer one of the dresses before he died?"

"Yes. You knew they had a thing, right?"

"Yes, I knew that." Jeffer had made it sound like a rather insignificant thing, though maybe it wasn't. "Do you know which dress he had? Did he have Wilma's dress or Dorothy's?"

"That I don't know. We only talked about it once or twice." He eyed me suspiciously. "He never talked to you about the dress? Ever?"

"No. We never talked about the dress. We never talked about anything in the memorabilia collection."

"Collection implies something much more deliberate. I think Jeffer only had a few things. Most of which were stolen."

"Stolen?"

"Well, eventually the studios became much more aware of

the value of things. Even if you took things out of the garbage, they'd still call them stolen just to get them back."

"So, where is this collection or whatever you want to call it?"

"I don't know. I assumed you knew."

"Other than the dress, do you think there's much that's worth anything?"

"Even if there is, there may not be. You have to be able to prove provenance for these things. You can't just show up with Judy Garland's gingham dress from *The Wizard of Oz* and not say how you got it."

"So, the blue dress, Dick Congdon got it from the trash, then gave it to Jeffer. If I can find it, then it has a clear chain of ownership."

"Exactly. So it's worth something."

"You said you don't know how Wilma got Dorothy's dress. Could it have been the dress Anthony had?"

"You think Wilma Wanderly killed Anthony?"

"She wouldn't have killed him herself. But she might have paid someone to do it."

"She'd have to make up a story about how she got the dress."

"I think that might be Miss Wanderly's specialty."

Walking out of Robert's apartment, I struggled to understand what I'd just learned. The idea that Wilma Wanderly might have had Anthony Mercer killed did make sense. She'd spent all those years in Vegas, after all, and had to know her share of Mafia types. One of them could have easily set her up with a contract killer.

Thinking that brought me to a stop in the courtyard. Wilma Wanderly was so sweet and charming in all of her films. She would never have made a movie where she hired a hit man, so how could she do that in real life? Well, that was a silly thought. I'd rubbed elbows with enough celebrities to know they were seldom anything like their screen personas.

Tina, who lived next door to Robert, called out through her open door, "Noah? Noah is that you?"

I wasn't sure I was in the mood for this, but I couldn't just walk away. I walked over to her door and said, "Yes, it's me."

"Come in for a minute."

Tina's apartment was a mirror of Robert's. She'd floated a sofa in the middle of her living room, and in front of it had put the largest coffee table she could find. Her entire life revolved around that coffee table. There was a stack of ten or twelve screenplays in one corner, a gray Powerbook 100, a couple of stained coffee cups, an over-flowing ashtray, tiny photos of her family and a couple of handmade Mexican dolls, mementos from when she lived in Mexico and wrote movies for minimum wage. She'd written them in English, which meant the translator got the screen credit—or, at least, that's the way she tells it.

She was curled on the sofa in a pair of Laura Ashley flannel pajamas, with her blond hair down and flowing over her shoulders, smoking a cigarette, and with two open scripts in front of her. She worked as a professional reader for one of the mega-agencies in town. She read scripts so that the people who made decisions about them didn't have to.

"I was going to call you. I spoke to Judith."

"Judith is speaking to a lot of people these days."

"I just want you to know that I had no idea. And I would have been much kinder if I'd known that you were sick too."

"I'm not sick, though. I'm HIV-positive. That's not the same as being sick." Well, at least not until you started taking AZT. And as if to emphasize that point, my stomach rumbled uncomfortably.

"You know what I mean, Noah."

"No, actually, I don't. And I'm not sure you know what you mean."

She decided to ignore that. Next to her on the sofa was her black cat, Thurgood, curled into a ball and snoozing away. She stroked him and said, "That's why you're here, to talk to Robert, isn't it?"

"No, it isn't."

"So he doesn't know?"

"I don't know what he knows. Maybe Judith called him, too. I didn't ask."

"Judith said you accused Jeffer of infecting you knowingly. He really couldn't have—"

"I didn't *accuse* anyone of anything. She's making it sound like I stood up in the middle of the restaurant and started pointing at people. I simply told the truth. Jeffer knew."

"But how could he—"

"I'm not sure he was always honest with himself, no less me. I'm sure he at least wanted to believe the lies he told."

"That sounds so terrible."

"You do know he was never good with the truth."

"No, he wasn't. I just never thought it mattered."

"Well, it did."

———

I'd snuck home a copy of *The Addams Family* and wanted to watch it. I didn't usually bring home new releases, it wasn't good for business and it was worse to bring them home on a Saturday night, but it had already been a strange enough day by the time I slipped out of Pinx that I felt I deserved it.

But when I got home, instead of curling up in the tiny loveseat in my tiny living room and watching the movie, I found myself dragging one of the dining chairs into the bedroom and pulling down three cardboard boxes I'd shoved into the built-in cabinets above my closet. These were pretty much all I had left of Jeffer Cole, and much of it I only had because I haunted the alley behind our house and snatched things out of the trash when his family threw them away.

I dumped the boxes onto my bed. They were filled with the most useless things: I had every cancelled check from our joint checking account; I had six or seven notebooks from classes Jeffer had taken in college; I had a couple of his sketch books; his Day Runners from 1987, 1988 and 1989; a thick stack of greeting cards he'd gotten from friends over the years; and a few other random odds and ends.

I stood for a moment staring at it all, then asked myself honestly, *What was I looking for?* If there actually *was* a collection of memorabilia, then it had to be stored somewhere. Since I no longer owned our house, it definitely was not hidden in the attic or boxed up and pushed into the crawlspace. Had it been, his family would already have found it. Yes, they might have missed it, but I trusted that their greed made them thorough.

So, had Jeffer borrowed part of a friend's garage or attic or cellar? He might have. That meant I was looking for a likely candidate or a written reference to the favor. Of course, he might also have rented a lockup somewhere. So I was also looking for a cancelled check to a storage facility or a key to a lock.

I started with the least likely items. I picked up his sketchbooks and, one at a time, flipped through them. Some of the sketches were good. Mostly they were ideas for sets he was working on or costumes, but a few were done for the joy of sketching. One was the view from our living room. *I could frame that,* I thought. And I might, someday—if thinking about Jeffer and our life together ever became comfortable.

The first few sketchpads failed to provide anything truly interesting. There were no scribbled notes referring to the address of a storage facility, and no keys taped to the back of a set rendering. Of course, there wouldn't be. Not if Jeffer wanted me to have whatever he'd collected. If he wanted me to have the collection he'd have found a way to tell me—

Wait, did Jeffer want me to have it? Yes, he must have. He'd left me everything, so he'd have wanted me to have the memorabilia—right? That might have been easier to believe if he'd actually ever mentioned it to me.

I was going through the last sketchbook, deciding that I might move on to the cancel checks next, when a letter fell out. It was addressed to Jeffer at his apartment on Cahuenga. The one he'd lived in when I met him; the one I'd moved into with him.

I took the letter out of the envelope and scanned it quickly. It was obvious the person was in love with Jeffer, he said so several times. Toward the end of the letter was the line, "I know you think you love this boy, but it won't last. It's doomed from the start." The letter was signed simply: Dick. I looked at the envelope again. The return address was D.C. Nothing else. No street. No city. Just D.C. Dick Congdon.

The letter itself wasn't dated, so I looked at the postmark. At the edges of the circle it said HOLLYWOOD, CA 90028. Inside was the date. MAY 13, 1987. That was the most disturbing thing about the letter. The date. Jeffer and I had been together for nearly a year. I was practically supporting him while he got his career moving. Why was Dick Congdon sending him a love letter? Had they been seeing each other? Had we overlapped?

I scanned through the letter again and didn't see anything that suggested they'd been seeing each other. Dick certainly could have carried a flame for that long. Or maybe they were still involved. It wouldn't have been hard for Jeffer to hide it from me, I was only a naïve twenty-two. Hell, it was never hard for Jeffer to hide things from me. My age didn't have much to do with it.

I took everything and stacked it on the floor next to the bed. I'd had enough. I wasn't looking at anything else. In fact, I grabbed my comforter, dragged it into the living room, made myself comfy on the loveseat, and watched *The Addams Family*.

5

"It's about a blue dress," I said as soon as I got downstairs. It was nine thirty, but I'd been up since five. Louis and Marc were busy setting up the table. There was already a tremendous amount of food: two-dozen muffins, several quiches, pounds of crisp bacon, biscuits, gravy, some kind of egg casserole.

I was gaping at it all when Louis asked, "What blue dress?"

"One of the blue dresses from *The Girl From Albany*."

"Wilma Wanderly and Dorothy Caine?" Leon asked. "God, I haven't thought of either one of them in decades."

He was not actually helping set up. Instead, he was leaning up against the building sipping a mimosa. He wasn't being as awful as it might seem, though. With Marc and Louis it was sometimes best to just stay out of the way and lend an encouraging word here and there.

"I met her yesterday. Wilma Wanderly," I explained.

"Wilma Wanderly? You *met* Wilma Wanderly?" Leon asked.

"Yes. She came by in her limo."

"You lucky dog. There isn't a drag queen in the city who wouldn't rip your eyes out for the chance to meet Wilma Wanderly."

I didn't feel all that lucky, but I smiled anyway.

"She thinks I have the dress from *The Girl From Albany*."

"Why on Earth does she think that?" Marc wanted to know.

"It has to do with Jeffer. It's a long story."

"Mimosa? Coffee? Both?" Louis wanted to know.

"Do you have any tea?"

"Absolutely. Herbal?"

"Please."

Louis disappeared into their apartment. I looked at Marc and said, "What's going on?"

"Brunch."

"Yes, I know, but that's a lot of food for just the four of us."

"Well, we've invited a few other people."

Oh. That was disappointing. I just wanted to sit around with the boys discussing everything I'd learned the day before. Meeting people was the last thing on my mind.

"So here's something I've been thinking about," Leon said. "Why kill Anthony? Why not just bonk him on the head and steal the dress?"

"Provenance," I said.

"Oh, well, that explains everything," Leon said sarcastically. "What in God's name does provenance mean?"

"Leon, behave," Marc admonished.

"If Anthony were alive you couldn't sell the dress," I said.

"Of course you could. That swap meet on Western, half the stuff in there was shoplifted from Nordstrom's and Bullock's."

"That's true, if all you want is a hundred bucks," I said. I knew that Leon was being deliberately contrary to get a rise out of me. I wasn't going to let that happen. "The dress is worth at least twenty-five thousand, though. Maybe more. I don't think Anthony was killed for a hundred bucks."

"You do have a point," Leon said grudgingly.

"In order for the dress to be worth that much you'd have to explain how you got it. If Anthony were alive he could tell people the dress was stolen. And then nobody would buy it."

"So, whoever has the dress is just going to make up a story explaining how they got it?" Marc guessed.

"Yes, I'd say that's the plan."

Louis came out with a cup of orange-flavored herbal tea for me. He'd put at least two teaspoons of honey into it, and a couple of Mint Milanos balanced on the saucer. Obviously, he was trying to fatten me up.

"This is a lot of food," I said to Louis. "Did you invite everyone from your office?"

"No one told you? Leon had the most brilliant idea."

We turned to look at Leon who said, "I know, I was surprised too. Anyway, I've invited people from the shows Anthony did business with so we can ask them questions. Originally, I was just hoping we could find out who Anthony's blind date was."

"And who set up the date," Marc added.

"Now we need to ask about the blue spangled dress."

"What time is everyone supposed to be here?"

Louis glanced at his watch. "In about five minutes."

"Oh my God," I said. I was tempted to run back upstairs and rework my hair. I'd tamed it into an S-shaped swoop, but I had the feeling it had come completely undone simply walking down the steps from my apartment.

"Speaking of dates, how was yours the other night, Leon?" Marc asked.

He groaned. "Heterosexuality never looked so good."

"What does that mean?" I asked.

"It means another date like this and I'm going to start dating women. It was horrid...this boy was the epitome of machismo. He picked me up in a truck—a goddamn truck—and then took me country and western dancing. He refused to buy me anything but a long neck beer, and then, we're dancing and he wouldn't let me lead, even after I told him I get motion sickness going backward all the time. Worst of all, he hadn't told me we were going dancing, so I was wearing the wrong shoes. No one can two-step backward in a pair of Converse high-tops. It's just not possible."

Suddenly, someone screamed on the other side of the courtyard. A knot of four men stood near the stairs, one of them wore a dark green caftan.

"Oh my Lordy! A memorial brunch! Anthony would have adored it!"

Leon stepped forward, "Ford! How are you?" Under his breath he said to me. "Ford Wheeler. *The Service*. Hour-long procedural about the Secret Service. Mondays at ten."

"I know Ford," I whispered back.

"Oh, do you?" He gave me a look. "Ford, these are my friends Marc and Louis. And, of course, you know Noah."

"Hello. Hello. Um, yes." Ford adored Jeffer, but did not care much for me.

"Ford, who are your friends?" Leon asked.

"These are my assistants. They have names but I never remember them. Is that a pitcher of mimosas? I'm dying of thirst. If I didn't know better I'd think I spent last night crawling across the Mojave."

Two of his assistants said, "You did."

And then, before Ford got his hands on the mimosa pitcher, another designer came up the stairs, then another. Soon, the courtyard was brimming with chatter, chatter that was punctuated by Ford's shrill voice saying, "Oh my Lordy! I haven't seen you in ages, darling."

I stood at the edge of the party, trying not to be noticed. In addition to Ford, I'd already met a couple of the other designers. I didn't want to mingle for fear of getting pulled into conversations about Jeffer.

Louis came over to me with a plate of food. "Here, eat this."

"Oh. I don't know if I can." I'd eaten both of the cookies he'd given me and felt a little full.

"Well, just hang onto it. You'll look like you belong."

"I'm not great at parties." And this one was a minefield.

"Don't think of it as a party. Think of it as a group interrogation. You need to be asking questions about Anthony's murder." He raised an eyebrow toward Ford and walked away.

I took a small bite of the spinach quiche. It was delicious. Then I put down the plate and tried to casually wander over to where Leon was chatting with Ford Wheeler.

"I am in love with Bill Clinton," Ford said. "You know he's friends with Linda and Harry."

"I adore *Designing Women*," Leon said.

"I'm lending a hand with some jackets they're having made for the campaign. You know, trying to find an in. I would kill to work on that show," Ford said. "I do get tired of nothing but blue suits week after week."

Leon noticed me hovering. "Well, this is a memorial so we have to gossip about the deceased. What do you know about Anthony's murder?"

"I don't know anything about Anthony's murder," lowering his voice. "I assume it's a black thing. They're always killing each other."

Leon frowned at him, "Darling, that's a little racist, even for me."

Ford rolled his eyes. "Whatever."

"So, tell me everything you know about Wilma Wanderly."

"Oh Lordy! Is she still alive?"

"Yes, of course, she is," one of Ford's assistants said, showing off. "She almost won an Emmy last year. Or was it the year before? She played the mother on that show. Oh, you know, the one. The show where the guy who isn't good at anything suddenly drinks this potion and then he's good at everything. She was the mom for three episodes."

"No darling, that was Maryanne Carver."

"It was?"

"Yes."

"Why on Earth are we talking about Wilma Wanderly?" Ford asked. "You don't think she killed Anthony, do you?"

"Apparently, she's trying to find a dress from *The Girl From Albany*."

"Oh, she's been after that dress forever. Keeps accusing everyone of having it."

"So you don't think Anthony had it?"

"Oh Lordy, no. That dress is in a landfill somewhere with the rest of the nineteen forties."

Suddenly, the party went completely silent. The only sound

was the classical music coming from Marc and Louis' boom box. Everyone was looking toward the top of the steps, so I looked that way too. Standing there was a short, stocky, fireplug of a guy wearing a black T-shirt and black jeans. He'd had his hair shorn off but wasn't bald. I recognized him, of course.

Billy Martinez.

Then, slowly, people began talking again. And several ran over to fawn over Billy. I assumed people had gone quiet because it was well known that Billy and Anthony didn't like each other. I sidled over to Leon and said, "I thought you only invited people from shows Anthony worked on. That's Billy Martinez from Hollywood Costume who just walked in."

"Is it? Well, apparently word spread," he replied.

"How do you know Ford Wheeler? I thought you did something with international film sales?"

"I have a friend who works in casting. I've been running into Ford at parties for years. Besides, I'm a very friendly person. Oh, look more people are here…" Leon said, even as he hurried off.

At that point, I drifted away. The chairs from the table had been lined up against Marc and Louis' living room wall, so I grabbed an empty one and sat down. The party suddenly seemed like an animal, a beast, a thing that bayed and snarled and roared in turns. More people came. And then more.

Near me, people were talking about Ross Perot. "Really I think his ears are perfectly normal. They draw him in cartoons like he's Dumbo. Which I think is awfully partisan. If they gave him more respect he might actually win."

I got up again and felt a little wobbly. I probably did need some more food. I'd had a slice of toast with my morning pills, and the two cookies and a nibble of quiche. I needed more than that. I squeezed my way over to the buffet table, picked up a plastic plate and tried to pick out something I could stomach. I decided I'd try the egg casserole, a little bit of fruit and a slice of bacon. As I picked out my food, an older woman with dyed black hair and dressed in black—looking more like Morticia Addams than she probably realized—was saying, "It's odd.

People keep bringing up Wilma Wanderly and everyone's acting like they never met her. I'll admit it. I worked with her when I first started out."

The man she was talking to—who was very short—looked up at her enraptured and nodded furiously.

She continued, "It was for one of her Vegas shows. I did the beading on the bodice of this fuchsia-colored dress."

"Oh my God, it *was* the seventies," said the short man.

"Yes, I said it was the seventies. Anyway, we ended up doing several fittings. She was very pleasant. But, the thing was, her son was always around, like a shadow. And the way she treated him; it was painful to watch."

Billy Martinez leaned into their conversation and said, "Are you talking about Albert Wanderly? Isn't he the creepiest? We dressed his mother for that pilot she did, *Old Broads*. You may not have heard of it. The network thought it would be a great idea to replace *Golden Girls* with basically the same show. It was hid-de-ous! Anyway, Albert had a crush on that girl who worked for me, Loraine. The tall one. You've seen her, poor thing. People called her Lurch behind her back. Well, I called her Lurch behind her back. Anyway, Loraine kind of liked Albert, but then Wilma went out of her way to talk her out of liking him. What kind of mother does that?"

A voice behind me asked, "How on Earth did this happen?"

I turned around and there were Robert and Tina. He wore a black turtleneck and a jean jacket, while she had on a black sleeveless, drop-waist dress, with an extra-small men's white T-shirt underneath and a black shawl. There were still morning clouds in the sky so it was only in the seventies, but it would be well into the eighties before we knew it. They were overdressed, like half the people there. As though they refused to trust the weather and had to prepare for a sudden frigid dip.

Tina stepped forward and kissed me on the cheek. "How are you, Noah?"

"I'm fine, thanks."

Robert looked at her like she'd gone mad and then asked

me, "Why are you having a memorial for Anthony? You barely knew him."

"My neighbors set it up."

"Did they know him?"

"Robert, stop it," Tina said. "I think we should be glad someone's doing something for poor Anthony." I was certain Tina had never met him.

"Actually, my neighbors are trying to get information about the night he was murdered. He was supposedly going on a date, and then there's the whole thing about the dress."

"Are your friends policemen?" Robert wanted to know.

"Amateur detectives."

"How ridiculous."

I said to Robert, "Your boss is here." I pointed to the spot where he'd been telling the story of poor Loraine, but he had vanished.

"How did you end up here?" I asked, to change the subject.

"Phone call. Apparently there's some kind of phone tree."

"All you have to do is say free booze and half the city comes running," Tina said.

"Speaking of which, we should get a mimosa before they run out," Robert said.

"Why don't you get one," Tina said. "And bring one back for me."

It was obvious he was being dismissed, and from the look on his face he knew it. Reluctantly, he walked away.

"I wish you would tell Robert what's going on with you," Tina said, as soon as he was out of earshot.

"Why haven't you told him?"

"It's not my place."

"But it was Judith's place to tell you?"

"She was wrong to do that. I think she was trying to hurt you, to be honest."

"That would certainly be in character."

"And besides, you and Robert used to be such good friends. He really should hear it from you."

Just then, I saw Willow and a gangly boy come up the stairs.

She was again wearing too many clothes. She'd pulled a pair of Daisy Dukes up over a pair of black stretch jeans pegged at the ankle, wore a men's white shirt with loose French cuffs and on top of that a pink tube top. For shoes she'd chosen a pair of pink Jellies. It was a bizarre look, but not too far out of step with the rest of the crowd. The young man with her was possibly still a teenager if the scruff on his chin was any indication.

"I have to talk to these two," I told Tina, then walked over to Willow. Tina tagged along, despite that I hadn't encouraged her.

"This is Kerry," Willow said, after I said hello.

"Hi, Kerry. I'm Noah and this is Tina."

"Yeah," he said in greeting.

"He feels really bad about Anthony," Willow said.

"Yeah."

To Tina I said, "Willow and Kerry were Anthony's assistants."

"Oh, well, I'm sorry for your loss," she said.

"Thank you," Willow said. Kerry looked concerned and a bit lost.

"Say, Kerry, do you remember, did you get sent home early the night Anthony died, like Willow?" I asked, cringing because I was being so obvious.

But Kerry just said, "Yeah."

"Do you have any idea who Anthony had a date with?"

"Yeah."

"You do?"

"He's afraid to say, though," Willow helped out. "Is the food any good?"

"Delicious. Why? Why are you afraid?"

"There's a rumor it was a Mafia hit," Willow interjected.

"Yeah," Kerry agreed.

"Do you know his date's name?"

"No."

"He doesn't know the guy's whole name. He heard Anthony call someone Brick on the phone. We don't know anyone named Brick."

That was interesting. Anthony had a date with someone named Brick. Something else occurred to me.

"You haven't figured out if anything's missing yet, have you?"

Willow shook her head and looked longingly at the buffet.

"Do you know if the dress from *The Girl From Albany* is there?"

"The blue sequined one?"

"Yes, that's the one."

"I guess. I'd have to check, but I don't remember seeing it lately."

"If it's not there, it might be what was taken,'" I suggested.

Just then, Robert came back carrying two mimosas. He glanced at Willow and Kerry and said, "Oh, hello."

Kerry whispered something to Willow and she said, "Yeah, he's the guy who works at Hollywood Costume." Then they both looked uncomfortable.

Having pity on them, I suggested, "You should go get something to eat."

Even before they were gone, Robert asked, "Why were you talking to Anthony's minions?"

"Something important just happened, didn't it?" Tina asked.

"I think it might have," I said, suddenly very tired. Sleep, I needed to get more sleep. Thinking I might tell the boys I had to go upstairs for a while, I turned, looking for them, and instead found myself staring at Javier O'Shea. He'd obviously just arrived and stood a few feet away staring at me.

Black hair brushed back, eyes maple syrup brown, his loose gray T-shirt clung to his chest and shoulders. He had his hands shoved into a pair of pleated khakis. He looked perfect; more like a model than a policeman.

And that's when I passed out.

6

WHEN I CAME TO, I WAS UPSTAIRS LYING ON MY FUTON BED with four men hovering around me: Marc and Louis, Leon, and Detective Javier O'Shea. I was very tempted to say, "And you were there. And you. And so were you." But their dour expressions told me they wouldn't appreciate the joke.

"Do we need to get you to the hospital?" Louis asked.

"Don't ask him, Louis. Just call 911 like I've been telling you to for the last five minutes," Marc said.

"I'm fine. Really. I think I might just be anemic." My doctor had warned me it might happen with AZT. The good thing was no one ever thought anemia was as serious as it was. "I have a doctor's appointment next week, okay? If it keeps happening I'll move it up."

"If you pass out again, I'm calling 911."

"I'm fine."

"You're sure?" O'Shea asked.

"Yes, I am."

"Really, you're all such drama queens," Leon said. "It's just a play for attention. Isn't it, darling?"

"You know me, just an attention whore."

Just then someone downstairs got to the boom box and switched it to a top forties station, playing something that was probably called "Jump" since that's the only word I could decipher.

Louis poked Marc and said, "We have guests. We should go back down."

"All right."

They started to leave the room, when Louis said, "Leon."

"Oh, right. Coming."

And then I was alone with O'Shea.

My bedroom is small with only enough room for my queen-sized platform bed and a set of makeshift shelves as a headboard. Four grown men standing around it had felt oppressive; yet, now that it was just O'Shea standing there—it felt even more so.

"What's going on downstairs, I didn't do any of that. It was all Marc and Louis."

"I'm not angry. Do you think I'm angry?"

He sat down on the bed. For a moment, I could barely speak. "Um, I think you have every right to be. Angry."

He had gotten angry with me in the past for meddling, well, meddling and nearly getting myself killed.

"Brunch seems harmless enough. And if you boys find anything out you're going to share it with me. Right?"

"How did you find out about it?"

"A couple of the people I interviewed yesterday are here. They mentioned it. So, what have you found out?"

"Since I saw you yesterday?"

Hmm. Thinking it through, all I'd really done was watch the movie that had the blue dresses in it, visit a couple of old friends, and shuffle through some of Jeffer's things only to find out he might have been seeing his old boyfriend months after we got together. I hadn't exactly been productive.

"I haven't found out much, to be honest. I think Jeffer did have the blue dress. At least, at one point. I've been trying to figure out if he stored it with a friend or if he used a storage facility."

"The dress is kind of famous. I've been asking about it." It felt weird to have him sitting on the bed, so I said, "You should go downstairs and talk to people."

"Yeah, I should. Can I ask you something?"

"Sure."

"Why do they all have to be so…uh, gay?"

"They are gay."

"I know, but not everyone's like that. You're not like that; I'm not like that. Your friends…well, your friends are kind of like that."

"I can be like that, too. Sometimes."

"Can you?"

"Sure. It's not a big deal. They're just being who they are."

"And I'm being an asshole? Noticing things like that?"

"Um, no, not really," I admitted. "You live in a world where that matters."

"And you don't?"

"I run a gay business in a gay neighborhood. My mother knows who I am and she's mostly cool with it. I don't have to deal with the things you do."

"Coming out is harder than I thought it would be," he said. "And I've hardly started."

I felt bad for him. I didn't know what he wanted from me, but was pretty sure I wouldn't be able to give it.

Louis came back in. In his hand was what looked like a milk shake. "Here, drink this."

"What is it?"

"It's a protein shake. Fruit, ice cream, protein powder."

"Where did you get protein powder?" He had a lot in his kitchen, things I'd never dreamed of, but I doubted he'd just happen to have protein powder lying around.

"I got it from the bodybuilder in number four." That was our straight neighbor who spent most of his time at the gym. We all agreed he'd gone too far, that his muscles were too big, but that didn't stop us from ogling him as he came in and out of the building.

"That was nice of him."

"Not really. I had to give him five bucks."

Shit. Now I had to drink it all. It didn't taste too bad. And I had to be thankful that Louis hadn't run out and bought some iron-rich calf's liver to pulverize. Ignoring the fact that I really didn't want the drink, I swallowed almost half of it.

"Thank you," I said.

Then I decided it would be a good idea to get out of bed. I was afraid Louis was about to run downstairs again and I'd be left alone with O'Shea, basically in my bed. I scrambled to the edge and then headed out to the living room with my smoothie in hand. I kept sipping at it, hoping to make it go away. The party was quieter, it seemed to be winding down.

"People are leaving. I hope that's not my fault," I said. Medical emergencies tend to put a damper on social occasions.

"I need to get down there," Louis said, before scooting out.

"I think we should go downstairs, too," I said to O'Shea.

"Um, sure, I guess."

He was hovering around me, the way guys do when they have things on their mind, sex things. I really needed to get away from him. If I hesitated too long he might—

I bolted out my door. Marc and Louis were waving off the last of the guests, while Leon had already pulled a chair over to the decimated buffet. Turning back to the courtyard, Louis saw that I was almost finished with the drink.

"Let me know how that sits. We may have found a way to get some nutrition into you."

"Do you have a bad stomach?" O'Shea asked.

"Ulcer," I lied. "That's why I'm a little anemic."

"You know, the Chinese swear by white rice." Leon suggested. "A small bowl before bed is supposed to help."

"Really?"

He shrugged, a little drunk. "I know. I thought white rice was all they ate."

Marc pulled out a chair from inside their apartment and the five of us sat down around the iron table, which was still stacked with scrapped-out dishes and picked-over platters. Say what you want about that crowd, they had healthy appetites. Louis brought out the very last bottle of champagne and filled everyone's glass, except for mine and O'Shea's. He was technically working.

"So—what did we find out?" Louis asked, sipping his champagne.

"Apparently," Marc began. "Wilma Wanderly has been asking everyone about the dress for weeks. And, she stopped by to see Anthony about it a week or so before he was killed."

"So she knew that Anthony had one of the dresses," I said.

"Yes, that seems clear."

"What else?" Louis asked.

"The date Anthony was going on was with someone named Brick," I said. I glanced uncomfortably at O'Shea. I hadn't mentioned it upstairs when he asked if I'd found anything out. But then, he was sitting on my bed, so maybe I wasn't thinking straight.

"It shouldn't be hard to find someone named Brick," O'Shea said, making a note on a little pad he'd taken out.

"In Hollywood?" Leon asked. "Don't be so sure."

"If you eliminate soap opera characters and the actors who play them, he's probably right," I said, defending him, though I didn't know why.

"The date was a setup," Louis said. "It wasn't from the personals. A friend of his set them up. At least, that's what he told people."

"Which friend set them up?"

"That I don't know. No one seemed to know."

"Well, I got two phone numbers," Leon said.

"What phone numbers?" O'Shea asked.

"Dates." Leon narrowed his eyes and studied O'Shea. "You're just a gayby, aren't you?"

"A what?"

"Leon, he doesn't need to talk about—" I started.

"A gayby is someone who's just coming out."

O'Shea flushed a very dark red. So red, in fact, that I decided to save him. "So, Anthony was shot execution-style, right?"

"Yes. Mercer was shot in the back of the head with a small-caliber pistol. From the position of the body, he was on his knees when he was shot."

"Why do that to a person?" Marc asked.

"With that type of pistol the bullet is going fast enough to pierce the skull, but not necessarily fast enough to exit, so what happens is the bullet bounces around inside the cranium. It's appealing to professional killers because there's little blood splatter from the shot. Compared to most murder methods, it's relatively neat."

Marc looked a little green.

"Willow mentioned cleaning up, though. She made it sound awful," I said.

"Gross," Leon added. "She said it was gross."

"It's kind of relative," O'Shea said. "As I recall there was a puddle of blood maybe a foot across. And, of course, the body loses control so there were other fluids seeping onto—you guys really want to know all of this?"

"I think we get the drift," Louis said. "What Willow would think of as gross is pretty mild for you."

"Exactly."

O'Shea continued, "The important thing is that we think it was a hired killer. What we're not sure of is exactly why someone wanted Anthony dead."

"We know the answer to that," Leon said.

"We do?" I wondered.

"Yes, we talked about it earlier." To O'Shea he said, "It has to do with the value of the dress. The killer couldn't leave Anthony alive to report the dress stolen. This way, whoever had him killed can make up a story about how they got the dress."

"Like Anthony had given it to them weeks ago," Louis added.

"Yes."

O'Shea thought it through. "That's interesting. But as long as the murder investigation is open, whoever has the dress can't come forward."

"They may not have thought things through," Leon admitted.

"Most people who murder don't think things through," O'Shea said.

"So who do we think killed Anthony Mercer?" Marc asked.

"Brick," we all said at once.

"His blind date," Leon added, "a professional hit man? Oh my God, that's a great name for a movie. *Blind Date With a Hitman*. Noah, get ten copies, they'll rent like crazy."

I ignored him. "The real question is, who hired Brick? My guess is Wilma Wanderly."

"Hollywood Costume," Marc suggested.

"Wait, what's that?" O'Shea wanted to know.

"Billy Martinez, the owner of Hollywood Costume is trying to buy Anthony's costume shop. He could have had Anthony killed. Now he's practically the only costume shop in town."

"I'll check him out tomorrow."

"But Billy Martinez wouldn't have stolen the blue dress," Louis said. "Would he?"

"We don't know for sure the dress was stolen. We don't know for sure if it was even there," Marc pointed out.

"No," I said. "Willow was familiar with the dress. She said she 'hadn't seen it lately.'"

"Well somebody was looking for something," Louis said. "Didn't she also say the place was ransacked?"

"It was a mess. And I agree, someone was looking for something," O'Shea confirmed.

"We should put down Dorothy Caine as a suspect," Marc said.

"Why? Did someone say something?" I asked.

"Just that she's fallen on hard times. But think about it. If she sold the dress she didn't get much. So, maybe she's figured out how much a set is worth and feels she was cheated. She could have had Anthony killed just to keep Wilma from getting the dress."

"So, wait a second," O'Shea said. "This is like a card game, isn't it? Whoever gets the right pair wins the pot."

"Pretty much."

"Who do you think did it, Detective O'Shea?" Leon asked.

"I'm not really supposed to say."

"Well, this isn't official. This is a parlor game."

"Murder is always about sex or money. Until we find this Brick person it could still be a date gone wrong. The style of the murder suggests a professional, but it could also be something the killer saw on TV."

And then Louis stood up and said, "Well, it's nearly two o'clock. I suppose I should start dinner."

7

Monday morning I left a message for Mikey that I'd be coming in late. It wasn't a busy day so he would be just fine. I was feeling better, I'd spent the rest of Sunday alone, sipping ginger ale, eating crackers, and watching *Breakfast at Tiffany's*. I had to keep rewinding the movie because I kept falling asleep. And then I went to bed and slept on and off for ten hours.

Now it was time to take care of a few things. First, I had to call my insurance agent; something I thought would take a whole lot longer than it did. I told him my rates had been increased a ridiculous amount and asked about changing insurance companies.

"You could try that, but don't expect a whole lot," he said.

"Why not?"

"Well, I'm sure there's a reason your rates were raised. That's going to follow you. Whatever it is, it's a pre-existing condition. You can't *not* disclose it."

There was a tone in his voice, one that suggested I'd done bad things and deserved what was happening to me. And maybe that would have been fair if I'd gotten a DUI and we were discussing my car insurance.

"What about group insurance? What if I get insurance for everyone at Pinx Video?"

"How many people do you think that might cover?"

I calculated in my head. Mikey might want it. Missy and Lainey might both still be covered by their parents' insurance, I wasn't sure. And Carl and Denny, well, I think they got Medicare. So, that was two.

"At least six," I lied. Worst-case scenario I could hire more people, I told myself.

"That's going to be pretty pricey," the agent said. "I'll work it up for you though. How about I drop it in the mail?"

What kind of salesman drops things in the mail? I thanked him and hung up. This wasn't good. I had a small nest egg from my share of the equity in the house Jeffer and I shared. If I used that to pay for the insurance I could get through the rest of this year and part of next, barring any other kind of disaster. The money would go away a lot faster if I needed work on my car—which was now five years old—had to have a root canal, or, heaven forbid, I had to go home and take care of my mom for some reason.

Of course, I could also fire someone and put myself on a more regimented schedule. I did spend a lot of time at Pinx, I just didn't spend my time there on a set schedule. But, I couldn't face the idea of firing anyone. None of them deserved to be fired. They all contributed. And it certainly wasn't their fault I suddenly needed to double my income.

My phone rang and I jumped. The cordless receiver was sitting right next to me on the teak dinette table. I just stared at it. The only person who called me in the morning was my mother, but I'd just talked to her the other day so I had no idea who it was. I waited until the answering machine picked up and my message played.

"Hello, this is Tina. I just want to make sure you're okay. The way you passed out yesterday isn't good. So, just, please let me know that you're okay."

She hung up.

It seemed she wanted to be friends again, and I wasn't sure I was interested. A lot had happened. She'd been awful. So had

Robert. They'd egged each other on. But they hadn't known everything, so I guess I had to forgive them. Or did I? They certainly could have given me the benefit of the doubt. They could have said, 'Noah's a good guy. He must have a good reason for leaving Jeffer at a time like this.'

No, I wouldn't be calling her back, I decided. Not right now. Then I went and took a shower. After I dried off, I wrapped a towel around my head and hoped that when I took it off my hair would be magically and reliably styled.

Standing in front of the closet, Jeffer's things on the floor caught my eye. I sat down on the bed and decided to at least flip through the last year of cancelled checks to see if he'd ever paid a storage company.

We kept the checks in a shoebox. The account was opened in July of 1987. We'd been together nearly a year. We closed it between Thanksgiving and Christmas in 1990, so there were almost five years of checks. Before I began flipping through them, I decided to put them in order by date. It wasn't hard. They were already in sequential bundles of twenty-five held together with a paperclip. Quickly, I sorted them out by year and then by month and then—

There was an extra packet for 1990. An extra packet that was different. The check itself was the same color as ours, but it had just Jeffer's name on it. The rest of the checks were from the joint account we had with the entertainment credit union, the one we'd been able to join because Jeffer was a production designer. This bundle of checks belonged to an account Jeffer had all by himself at Security Pacific.

I flipped through the checks. They were in order and covered almost six months. Jeffer, or someone, had accidentally thrown them in with our joint account. They began in April 1990 with check number 1051 and continued until August 1990 with check number 1073.

Looking through, about half of the checks were to a Dr. Paganelli. I guess that made sense. Jeffer hadn't wanted me to know he was sick, so he'd used the account to pay for his doctor visits. The checks were for ten dollars each, so he was only paying his co-pay. He always had insurance through his union, IATSE.

I wondered for a moment how things might have been different if he'd been in my position and had to get insurance on his own. He would have had to tell me what was going on with him, I imagine. He would have had to be honest.

The checks that weren't to Dr. Paganelli were more random. There was one to a boutique on Melrose where Jeffer bought me a royal blue velvet suit jacket for my birthday. It does look good on me, but I've only worn it once—to dinner with Jeffer. I really don't have places to wear a blue velvet jacket. There were several checks for cash. Monthly, for forty-nine dollars, and a few others for larger amounts.

Where had the money come from? I wondered. Did the account still exist? Unfortunately, there were no statements in the shoebox for the credit union account or the Security Pacific one.

Forty-nine dollars sounded about right for a storage facility. Did he pay cash? Why wouldn't he write a check directly to the facility?

I doubt Jeffer knew that his family would make a grab for our things. So he must have thought I'd eventually find every-thing— including this secret account. Did he not want me to know about the storage facility? Did he not want me to know about the blue dress and whatever else he'd collected? Why wouldn't he want me to know? I put the checks back into the box. That was as much I could deal with at the moment.

It was drizzling outside—very unusual for June—and looked cold, so I put on a white turtleneck with a denim work shirt, my black jeans and my black-and-white checked Vans. On the way out of the apartment, I grabbed *The Addams Family*, then hurried down to my car. I stopped at the Mercado and got a dozen fresh churros, then headed to Pinx, promising myself I'd eat at least two churros, maybe three.

When I walked into Pinx, Mikey was sitting alone behind

the counter and there were two customers skulking about. He handed me a list of videos and I handed him the box of churros.

"What is this?" I asked.

"Those are the titles we rented this weekend from the Hidden Treasures shelf." Then he opened the box and said, "Oh, churros, yum!"

Pulling one out of the box he took a bite. I took one and bit into it. It should have tasted crisp and sugary, but instead all I could taste was the fat it had been cooked in.

"These are wonderful. From the Mercado on Sunset?"

"Yes. They are good." Or at least they used to be. I decided not to be churlish about the shelf, and said, "Congratulations on the success of Hidden Treasures. I'm going to work on time cards."

"I already did that. And I filled out the checks, all you have to do is sign them."

I might have been annoyed by this, in fact, I should have been. He was doing my job for me and not even asking. But the extra time allowed me to ask something I'd been wondering about.

"Have you heard anything about the murder of costume designer Anthony Mercer?"

"I think a customer mentioned it. I don't really watch the news if I can avoid it. Too depressing."

"Well, the night he was killed Anthony was supposed to have a date with someone named Brick. Do we have anyone named Brick in the system?"

"You're not getting involved with another murder, are you? I mean, that would be a terrible idea."

It was a terrible idea and I knew it. It's just I felt like Anthony's murder was involving me much more than I was involving myself, even if only because everyone thought I had a blue dress. A blue dress worth killing for.

"I'm not involved. My neighbors were talking about it, that's all. So just out of curiosity, do we have anyone name Brick in the system?"

Mikey turned to the CRT and plugged in some search terms. "Brice, Byron and a whole lot of Brians, but no Brick."

"Okay. Thanks."

I slid the bag containing *The Addams Family* video toward him. He opened it up and as soon as he saw it said, "This was so great. 'Are they made from real Girl Scouts?'"

I smiled. "That was funny. This is random, but Dorothy Caine isn't one of our customers, is she?" Many of our customers were actors, a handful of whom were famous, so it wasn't really that random.

"No. But we have Jayne Van Hooten."

"Um, okay." Jayne Van Hooten was another actress from the same period, but I didn't see what her being a customer had to do with—

"Her sister," Mikey explained.

"Oh, that's right." Then I remembered, "Aren't they involved in some kind of feud?"

"They despise each other. But that doesn't mean Jayne wouldn't know where her sister is. And I can't imagine the feud would stop her from giving you her sister's address."

"All right, give me the address."

"Does this have something to do with the costumer's death?"

"Probably not," I said. It was a semi-honest answer. "So, you knew Jeffer pretty well. Did he ever mention that he had a collection of memorabilia?"

"No, he never said anything."

"Did he ever mention a dress from *The Girl From Albany*?"

"No. Is that why you want to talk to Dorothy Caine? It's about the dress?"

"Yes."

Apparently, he didn't consider that getting involved with murder, since he clicked the keys that would get me Jayne Van Hooten's address. And, of course, he wouldn't since I hadn't given him all the information.

"I have a collection," he said.

"You do?"

"Sure. We get three times as many posters as we can put up in the window. I take them home."

"Oh."

"I mean, I hope that's okay. You said to throw them out so I didn't think you cared."

"No, it's fine. I just never thought about it, that's all."

"It's hard to imagine that a poster from *Hudson Hawk* might someday be worth something, but you never know."

Jayne Van Hooten lived on Micheltorena in a butter-colored mansion that looked out over the north end of the Silver Lake Reservoir. The house was two stories, with decorative shutters painted a weathered tan. It sat on a large mound, lifting it high above the street and vastly improving its view. The mound was planted with icicle plants that hung over the retaining wall at street level, where there was also a garage and a gate in front of a flight of cement stairs leading up to the house. Next to the gate was an intercom system. I was going to have to think of a story. I doubted I could just ask for the information, no matter what Mikey thought. There was an actress killed a few years ago by a guy who just came to her door. The famous were a bit more careful these days.

I pressed the call button on the intercom and waited. Thirty seconds later a woman's voice came on and asked, "Who is it?"

"Hello. I am, um, trying to find Dorothy Caine. She has an overdue video and the information we have on her is out of date. Would you be able to—"

The intercom made a screeching sound and I grabbed the gate and opened it. I hadn't really expected it would be so easy to get in.

I climbed the steps up to the house. There was a lovely walkway that led to the front door, and beyond that a large terrace. Glancing over my shoulder, I saw that the view of Silver Lake was spectacular.

The wide front door opened before I got there and I found

myself face to face with Jayne Van Hooten. She was taller than I expected, painfully thin and somewhere around sixty-five. Her dyed-blond hair was coiled onto her head like a fuzzy snake.

"If that story's true about the video you can kiss it goodbye."

"I'm sorry, you don't know where your sister is?"

"Of course I know where she is. She's out back. What I also know is that she doesn't have your videotape. What was it? Some sex movie?"

I was beginning to feel protective of Dorothy, so I said, "*The Sound of Music*."

"Ha! No, it's not. Dorothy hates Julie Andrews."

"Why would anyone hate Julie Andrews?"

"She hates her because I like her. If I say white, she says black. It's been like that since we were kids. What are you really doing here?"

Telling Jayne anything was probably a bad idea. "It's kind of personal."

"Oh really? You're too little."

"I'm sorry?"

"She likes her gigolos to be big and strapping. You're neither."

I decided to ignore that. "If I could just see her for a couple of minutes."

Jayne shrugged. "I told you she's out back. You have to follow that path around the house." She pointed at some terra cotta tiles that had been set into the lawn.

I thanked her and started on the path.

"Be careful. The bitch bites."

I followed the tiles around the house. Most of the backyard sloped downward from the house. Attached to the house was another patio atop a berm. I didn't see anyone on the patio, so I continued down the back lawn. When I got around the patio, I saw there was a small red house tucked beneath some trees on the far side of the yard. The path continued to meander toward the house in twists and curls.

The house had a sliding glass door on the front, and a tiny deck. Attached above the sliding glass door was a white piece of wood cut in an abstract way. It looked like a bowtie drawn by a child. Next to the deck was a round pond, raised a few feet with a distinct lip going all around it. As I passed, I could see it was filled with lily pads and koi.

When I stepped onto the deck I saw the glass door was open, so I said, "Hello?"

I heard a crash and then Dorothy Caine rushed out onto the deck. She had a drink in one hand. With the other she brushed her hair out of her face. Dorothy had not aged as well as her sister, or Wilma Wanderly for that matter. She looked swollen, and I might not have recognized her if she hadn't used most of her makeup kit to draw the face she'd shown the world in the forties and fifties on top of the one she had now. The overall effect was kind of blurry.

"Who are you?"

"I'm Noah Valentine. I'd like to talk to you about the dress you wore in *The Girl From Albany*."

"I love that dress. You wanna buy it?"

"Do you still have it?" It would certainly change everything if she did.

"Sure I do. It's around here somewhere."

"Can I see it?"

She froze for a second, as though she'd come to a complete stop, and then started again. "My sister send you out here? She wants the dress, you know. Thinks I owe it to her." She flopped down into a deck chair rather ungracefully.

"I read somewhere you'd given up drinking."

"I have given it up. Mostly."

"And that you were just at Betty Ford."

She shrugged. "I couldn't afford a vacation, so I thought, why not? I love the desert. Do you want a drink? Is that why you brought this up?"

"Alcohol hasn't been agreeing with me."

"Alcohol agrees with me all the time."

I smiled at her because there wasn't much else to do. Then, I said, "You sold the dress, didn't you? Did you sell it to Wilma Wanderly?"

"Wilma? No. I didn't sell the dress to her. Did you see what she said about me on Barbara Walters? She said I couldn't handle fame. I mean, that's ridiculous. I can handle fame. What I couldn't do was cash in on it. I mean, a hundred dollars a week from a studio contract was a lot in 1950 but not enough to last a lifetime for God's sake. My sister, though, she always knew where the money was—men. Jayne married well, three times. Three. I married twice. Both trumpet players. I mean, what a joke."

"I think Wilma has the dress. Who'd she get it from?"

"I didn't sell Wilma the dress. She was an all right kid when we did the movie, but boy that didn't—"

"Who'd she get the dress from?"

"I need another drink. You want one? Have a drink with me."

I casually stood in front of the door, blocking her way. I wouldn't have tried to stop her. Probably couldn't have if she put her mind to it, she was taller and weighed more than I did. Not that she was thinking all that rationally.

"No, thanks," I said to the offer.

She sized me up. "Do you see where you are? Huh? Do you see where she put me? It's her idea of a joke."

"Whose idea of a joke? I'm confused."

"My sister's. Can't you see it? Look around."

I looked again at the small, red house with the odd standing pool nearby and the white bow—bone, it was bone. A doghouse. Jayne Van Hooten had built a doghouse and put her sister in it.

"You see it now, don't you?"

"I do."

"And people wonder why I drink."

I couldn't stand there and talk about sibling rivalry, as interesting as it might be. "Dorothy, someone I know was killed and I think it might have something to do with your blue dress."

She tried to focus on the idea of someone dying for her dress and then she said, "Bunny."

I almost looked out at the lawn looking to see if she'd seen a rabbit. "Bunny?"

"Bunny Hopper."

"The drag queen?"

"Yes, the drag queen. Who else is going to buy a used spangled dress?"

8

FEELING GUILTY ABOUT IGNORING PINX FOR MOST OF THE day, I went back and sent Mikey home early. He didn't want to go, even when I said I'd pay him for the full day. It took me nearly an hour to coax him into it, and at the end of all that he only left twenty minutes early.

I'd expected to spend most of the evening in the back working on our taxes, but Carl and Denny were having a spat so it seemed like a good idea to separate them. I had Carl in the tape room cleaning up and Denny out on the floor re-alphabetizing, while I sat at the counter dealing with the occasional customer.

Since I knew I wouldn't be getting home until nearly eleven and Marc and Louis would be fast asleep, I called them while I was at the counter.

"I talked to Dorothy Caine," I told Louis.

"He went and saw Dorothy Caine," he repeated for Marc. "What was that like?"

I could hear Marc in the background saying, "Was she drunk? I hear she's a drunk."

"She sold the dress to Bunny Hopper."

"She sold the dress to a drag queen," Louis told Marc. "Bunny Hopper."

"Is she still performing?" I wondered.

Louis was listening to Marc. Then Marc came on the line. "Noah, Bunny Hopper used to perform at the Queen Mary."

"In Long Beach?"

"No dear, in Studio City. The Queen Mary Show Lounge. The drag bar on Ventura."

"Oh." I'd never heard of it.

"She hasn't been there in ages, though. Hmmmmm, let me see. I have a light morning tomorrow. Let me see if I can find her."

"All right."

"I'll call you in the morning."

When I got home a couple of hours later, there were two fresh blueberry muffins wrapped in plastic outside my front door. From Louis, obviously. I ate half a muffin while watching *The Palm Beach Story*—which, I have to admit I chose from the Hidden Treasures shelf. I fell asleep part way through the movie, thinking how nice it would be to love a man so much I'd run off to marry a bespectacled millionaire just so I could make all of my true love's dreams come true. Sometimes movie logic made so much more sense than real life.

In the morning a suspicious package arrived.

Well, it was suspicious until I saw the return address was Grand Rapids. It was from my mother. Though I had no idea what she might be sending me.

After the delivery guy left—why do real life delivery men never live up to their gay porn counterparts?—I put the package onto the dinette table and got a knife to open the box.

Inside were old copies of *Photoplay* with Wilma Wanderly on the cover, *Life* from the sixties, and *People* from the seventies. There were also clippings, dozens of them, from newspapers, supermarket scandal rags and other periodicals. All told Wilma Wanderly's life story—her difficult, challenging life story.

Already a star, Wilma had married a much older man when

she was only seventeen. Two years later, her son Albert was born. Considering the dates given in the stories, I calculated Wilma's age at around seventy and Albert's as just past fifty. One of the clippings mentioned Wilma's claim that she'd lied about her age, and was actually thirteen when she began at the studio and just fifteen when she married. But it was common for older actresses to make claims like that in order to make themselves appear younger—though why two years would matter to a seventy-year-old woman was beyond me.

When Wilma was just twenty-two (or twenty, depending on what you believe) her husband dropped dead on a Hollywood street. It was later determined he died of a fractured skull. Wilma claimed she had no idea how this might have happened, though there were rumors of a terrible row a few days before, a heavy crystal ashtray and a maid who was given a small house in Glendale by the studio. The young widow swore off marriage, though she was often shepherded around Hollywood by young, attractive up-and-comers.

In the late fifties when she was in her mid-thirties, her career began to falter and she went to England to make a series of films with director Terrance "Scotty" Scott. She fell desperately in love with her married director and after the second film they made together had a child by him who tragically only lived for eight days. Scotty stood by her, though somehow forgot to divorce his wife, and there was a second pregnancy that ended in a miscarriage while they were making their final picture together. The films were, in retrospect, mediocre. But due to the scandal that swirled around them, quite profitable.

It was after this that Wilma reinvented herself as a Las Vegas headliner. She spent nearly two decades singing in smoky lounges backed up by nearly naked chorines. In the early Vegas years, she was romantically linked to several mob figures, like Gianni "The Rat" Agnotti and Big Jim Perelli. Then throughout the eighties she was semi-retired, appearing occasionally in guest roles on sitcoms and even a few times on game shows, working just enough to meet her eligibility requirements for SAG insurance.

After I read through everything in the box, I called my mother. "Hi Mom, I got the package."

"Already? That's so fast."

"You sent it Priority Overnight."

"And that means it gets there fast?"

"Yes, they make it a priority."

"Oh, well that makes sense."

"Where did you get this stuff?"

"The basement."

"Do you keep information on everyone in Hollywood?"

She laughed at the idea. "Oh no, don't be silly. Just Elizabeth Taylor, Bette Davis, Wilma Wanderly and little Natalie Wood." Since two of the four actresses were now dead, it didn't seem this would be a time-consuming pastime.

"Well, thank you. It's interesting stuff."

"Oh, I'm glad you like it. All right then, I'll talk to you this weekend."

"Mom, you can stay on the phone for a minute."

"Oh, no dear, we don't want to pay daytime rates. They charge a fortune."

"Just this once? Besides, you just paid a fortune to send me this package."

"Well, it's only been three days since we talked. There's really nothing to say. Oh, Carolyn took me to her church. It was fascinating."

"What kind of church was it?"

"Oh, I don't know. Christian of course, but specifically which kind I'm not sure. They like to raise their hands during the service. Carolyn says it's so God can touch them. I thought that was nice. All these people with their hands raised as though they were waving at God."

"Was God on the ceiling?" I asked.

"Oh now stop it. You know perfectly well God's not on the ceiling."

I did. But did they?

"How was the sermon?"

"Oh, it was lovely, just lovely. There were a few things that were, well, uncomfortable, and I did say so to Carolyn after-wards, specifically that you and Jeffer were never that kind of gay."

I didn't want to know what 'that kind of gay' was. I had an inkling, of course, and thought their preacher should probably mind his own business, but didn't see much point in bringing that up.

"Her daughter and son-in-law were there. They've got three little cherubs and another on the way. I like kids, but Carolyn does go on and on about them. She asks me every time I see her if I'm sad I won't ever be a grandmother."

"That doesn't seem very nice."

"Oh, I think she just forgets she's already asked me."

I doubted that. "Well, I'm glad you had a nice time."

"I did. Well, I should—"

"I watched *The Palm Beach Story* last night."

"Oh gosh, Joel McCrea. He was so handsome in that movie."

"He was."

"And Claudette Colbert. Oh, she was just lovely. Is she still alive?"

"I don't know. I think so. Do you remember *It Happened One Night?*"

I knew she loved that movie and I knew that if I got her talking about it I could keep her on the line, that we'd switch over to other Colbert films or even some of Gable's. I don't know why it was important to me that she stay on the line, other than the fact that it had been very kind of her to send me her Wilma Wanderly clippings. I promised myself I'd get them back to her when we figured out what had happened to Anthony Mercer.

Needless to say, I was nearly an hour later than usual getting to Pinx. I walked in the door and Missy said, "Someone named Judith called you. Twice."

"Okay, thanks," I said, as I slipped *The Palm Beach Story* onto the counter.

Missy took the video out of the bag and said, "How can you

watch black-and-white movies? They're, I don't know, just not real."

"Movies aren't real, Missy. Not even when they're in color."

"Oh, this goes over there, doesn't it?" She waved toward Mikey's Hidden Treasures shelf.

"It does. So, do you have everything under control?"

She gave me her patented 'Seriously' look and said, "Noah, it's not a hard job. And, like, there's no one even in here."

"There's something I need to deal with. I'll probably be gone for a couple of hours."

"Sure, whatever."

"I probably won't be reachable, so if you have a problem call Mikey."

"Yeah. If I have a problem I'll wait until you get back."

"Okay then," I said.

There was no way I was going to solve the whole Missy/Mikey problem so I decided to admit defeat and get on with things.

A few minutes later, I was back in my car and on the way to Judith's. She lived in Brentwood, which, from Silver Lake was a crosstown nightmare. I told myself it wouldn't be too bad—it wasn't rush hour after all—and put the cassette of *A Little Night Music* into the player. I took Vermont down to the 10 to cut across town, even though it probably wasn't any better than taking Sunset. It at least offered the possibility of speed. It took nearly forty minutes to get there, and I was listening to "The Miller's Son" when I pulled up in front of Judith's complex.

Her condo was on the third floor of a cream-colored stucco and redwood building, which had a couple of over-pruned trees in the front. She had a westerly view of the hills and sunsets. It was a nicely decorated unit that most people would have felt spoiled to live in. Judith and her husband felt desperately deprived, since most of the children Tiffany went to school with lived in multimillion-dollar estates and were driven to school by maids or nannies or even chauffeurs but almost never by their parents. The simple act of raising her own child in that neighborhood felt like poverty to Judith. And it mortified her daughter.

She buzzed me in, and by the time I got to her unit she was fuming. "I'm not speaking to you. You sent the police after me," she said while I was still in the hallway.

"Detective O'Shea was here?"

"Yes. It was terrible."

"He's a nice cop."

"Maybe to you. He wasn't nice to me."

"Were you telling him the truth? Sometimes cops get testy when you lie."

"Are you calling me a liar?"

"I met Wilma Wanderly. She offered me twenty-five thousand for the dress."

Judith shrugged, half acknowledging that she'd told me a whole lot of lies. "Did you want something to drink? Iced tea? Coffee?"

"I'm not staying long." I wanted to say my piece, go find some place to eat lunch, and then head back to Silver Lake before rush hour. I had to stay on schedule.

"She'll pay more than that, you know. We should work together and split the money."

"Why should I do that? It's my dress."

"So you've found it?"

"No. I really don't think it exists." Now I was lying to her. Well, she deserved it.

"I told Jasper about your stunt with the pills. He doesn't believe you're sick."

"I'm not sick. I don't have AIDS. I don't even have ARC. I'm HIV-positive."

"Yes, well, he doesn't believe you're that."

"Does he think I borrowed the pills?"

"He thinks that if Jeffer really infected you that you would have had him arrested and thrown in jail."

"Well that's Jasper. I couldn't put someone I loved in jail. I mean, by that point he could barely walk."

"We all think it's odd that you didn't say anything until now."

"Wouldn't that have just made a bad situation worse? Our friends would certainly have stopped seeing him. Jasper might have been kind enough to point out he was a felon. How would your parents have felt about it?"

"You could have told us after he died."

"You mean when you were trying to steal my home?"

"We might not have—"

"No, I think you would have."

She backed up like she'd been slapped. Then her face got hard. "Look, I meant what I said about the dress. If you want me to help you find it we can work something out."

I stood there a moment thinking things through. I now knew that Jeffer had been paying for a storage facility. Judith didn't know that. I wondered for a moment if she'd found any random keys when she was going through his stuff. Asking would oblige me to split the money with her, so I wasn't going to. Besides, if she'd found any keys I was pretty sure she'd have mentioned them by now.

"If I change my mind I'll let you know."

I was almost all the way back to Pinx, when I remembered that Marc was going to call that morning. I'd stopped at a mediocre Thai restaurant for lunch. The Thai Iced Tea had been yummy, but the Pad Thai was slightly off. I ate enough of it to take my pills and keep my stomach relatively settled. When I walked into Pinx, I asked Missy if Marc had called.

"Marc who?"

"He's a friend of mine. He said he was going to call this morning."

"No. He didn't call. Your friend Tina called, though. She was really nice."

I frowned.

"I'll be in the back. In case Marc calls."

"And if Tina calls?"

"I'm not here."

I assumed Marc's not calling meant he hadn't had much luck finding Bunny Hopper. And why should he? Los Angeles was a big place. You couldn't just find people the way you could in a small town. Except you could do just that.

L.A. is really a bunch of small places that overlap in different ways. Yeah, there were thirteen million people in the county, but if you're looking for a drag queen that number gets small fast. Maybe five percent of the city is gay. That's around six hundred thousand people, about the size of Columbus, Ohio— a Columbus of gay people. Subtract the lesbians and you're talking Cincinnati. Remove every guy who doesn't do drag for a living and, well, it's a pretty small town no one's ever heard of. All we had to do to locate Bunny was find someone else who lived in that same small town.

I fiddled with the bookkeeping for a while. I really wanted my 1991 taxes to go away. I was almost sure I didn't owe any money, or at least not much, but I had to get the paperwork right. Jeffer had done our taxes the first year we had the business. I'd managed to get through 1990 mainly because Jeffer had done three quarters of the year already.

I promised myself I'd get better at this aspect of my life. Really, it was just going to take a little determination and patience. It was, after all, only math. And relatively simple math at that. So, I was going to sit there until I'd made a serious dent—

The phone rang and I snatched it up.

"Pinx Video. Can I help you?"

"Noah?"

"Marc?"

"I know I said I'd call in the morning, but I learned an important lesson. Never, never try to call a drag bar first thing in the morning. They're not open until eleven thirty and they don't answer the phone until noon."

"Were you able to find Bunny Hopper?"

"Well, they wouldn't give out any information on her, but

they did take my number and promise to call her. I was sure they were just blowing smoke up my—

"Pinx Video. This is Missy."

"It's for me, Missy. Thanks."

She hung up.

"Anyway, guess who called me an hour later?" Marc picked up where he'd left off.

"Bunny Hopper."

"Yes. We have an audience at seven thirty."

"An audience?"

"Apparently she's the dowager Queen of Watts or some such."

9

Marc and Louis came by Pinx after they got home from work at about quarter to seven. I offered to let them rent a couple of videos on the house, but they swore they wouldn't have time to watch them. So I said goodbye to Carl and Denny —who were fortunately no longer fighting but were instead now sickly sweet—then we left and got into Marc's Infiniti.

"Shouldn't I drive?" I asked, though I really didn't want to. "We're going to Watts. We should take the worst car."

"Or the one with the best insurance," Marc said.

"Oh, okay, I hadn't thought about it that way."

"Zero deductible," Louis added.

I couldn't help wondering why was it so easy to insure cars but not people? We went around the block so we could get going in the right direction, then zigzagged down to take the 101 south.

"What did you mean Bunny's the dowager Queen of Watts?" I asked.

I expected Marc to answer, but it was Louis who said, "They're a rogue court in Watts."

"I don't know what that means."

"Have you heard of the Imperial Court System?"

"I guess not." I'd heard of the Imperial Valley and I assumed they had a legal system, but I didn't think that was what Louis was talking about.

"The Imperial Court is a drag court. There's one in Los Angeles, Long Beach, Orange County. They put on drag shows and raise money for charity. Every year there's a new emperor and empress."

Now it was Marc's turn. "Apparently, the queens in Watts had a falling out with the rest of the queens and formed their own court. That's how Bunny became the dowager queen of Watts."

"I see."

We merged onto the 110 south. Traffic wasn't terrible, but then I don't think many people were on their way from Silver Lake to Watts at seven on a Wednesday night. The signs started to display numbered streets: 99th, 101st, 106th. A part of the city I knew was there but was unfamiliar with.

Watts sits above the still-under-construction 105 between the 110 and the 710. It's about twelve miles south of Silver Lake and worlds away. We got off at Century Boulevard. Even after the recent riots, the neighborhood didn't look too bad. We only saw one burned-out building, a Trak Auto that had been boarded up. Graffiti had been painted on since the riots, gang symbols mostly, but taking center stage was FUCK THE POLICE 187.

"It's not too bad down here," Marc said, after we drove by the Trak Auto.

"The worst of the riots were northwest of here," Louis said.

The thing about a slum in Los Angeles is that you don't know you're there, at first. People still mow their lawns, touch up the trim on their windows, drive decent cars and water their lawns. It just doesn't look the way a bad neighborhood is supposed to look. Then, the deeper in you go, the worse it gets. First, bars appear on people's windows and doors. Then, cars get older and in need of repair, and the lawns start to die.

We found Zamora Avenue and the address that Marc had been given. It was a white house with green shutters and black wrought iron bars on the windows. The lawn was neat but dead.

Of course, we were in the sixth year of a drought so anyone whose lawn was green wasn't following conservation rules. Rules that were boldly ignored in the wealthy parts of town.

Marc clicked his key fob at the car after we got out and it beeped. We walked over to the gate that crossed the driveway. Louis gave me a look and raised an eyebrow, as though acknowledging the illicit thrill of being white people in the ghetto.

Rather than walk up to the front door, Marc continued back toward the garage. At first I thought we'd been told to come around the back, but then Marc walked up to the garage's side door and knocked. Inside, a man yelled, "Enter." Marc opened the door and we went in.

Converted garages are not uncommon in Southern California, whether permitted or not. This garage, though, had not been converted at all. It was an unfinished garage, with studs and cobwebs showing. Toward the back, was a queen-sized sleigh bed, a dormitory-sized refrigerator with a hot plate on top, a row of travel trunks—one of them with a portable television sitting on it—and a metal clothing rack. The rack was stuffed with clothes, mostly women's gowns. But it wasn't large enough to hang all of Bunny Hopper's wardrobe. No, around the garage hanging from hooks and nails hung the rest of her wardrobe in a rainbow of colors.

Directly across from us, Bunny Hopper sat upon a throne; a large, mahogany chair with lion's paw arms and a bouquet of roses carved into the backrest. She was small, her feet barely touching the ground, but she managed an unsurpassed regalness. Her cheeks were round, and she wore a gray wig that was parted down the center and pulled back severely into a bun. She looked like a black Queen Victoria. The satiny black dress she wore was decorated with several strands of fake pearls. Over the dress she wore a purple, ermine-lined cape—or more probably rabbit done up to look like ermine.

Her crown was gold-painted plastic, ruby-colored glass and more fake pearls. She held two scepters, both having once been broomsticks that were now spray-painted gold and encrusted at the top with glass ruby gems and plastic pearls. Next to Bunny, a tall, thin, very young black man curved over her like a palm tree in the wind.

The garage had a very odd, musty smell. There was the normal oily dirt smell of a garage, but it also smelled of sickroom. A smell I recognized from visiting Jeffer near the end. That explained why Bunny Hopper was no longer at the Queen Mary Show Lounge—and also why she was living in a garage.

We introduced ourselves and Bunny handed the scepters to her footman. Putting both hands on one knee, she leaned forward, gave us a bone-chilling stare, and in an imperious voice said, "You're here about the dress that Wilma Wanderly stole from me?"

"She stole it from you? Really?" I asked.

"Yes, she did."

"Did you call the police?" Marc asked.

"It wasn't that kind of theft."

"What kind of theft was it?"

Her glare hardened. "She paid my sister five thousand dollars to let her in here to snatch my dress. My sister never gave me a nickel of it either. Claims it's rent. Rent! Five thousand dollars to live in a garage. That's what I call theft."

"Wilma tried to buy the dress from you first, though?" I asked.

"Yes. I refused. I would never have sold that dress. I wanted to be buried in it. I don't think Dorothy Caine would have sold it to me if I hadn't planned to keep it."

"Wilma offered you five thousand dollars?"

"That was the first offer. Her second was better. My sister's not very bright, you see." She passed a chilly stare over the room then said, "Now, you'll answer a question for me. Why are you so interested in my dress?"

"My lover was Jeffer Cole," I explained. "Wilma Wanderly thinks he had one of the dresses. And she thinks he gave it to me."

"But he didn't?"

"No, he didn't."

"Well, that's curious."

"You wouldn't have any idea who might have told her that Jeffer had one of the dresses?" I asked.

"Why yes, of course. I did."

"Why do you think Jeffer had the dress?"

"In better times, I had my outfits made at Mercy Costumes. Anthony was a genius when it came to dressing a queen. One time I was in for a fitting and Jeffer was there. He and Anthony talked about the dresses they both had. I tried to buy one of them, but neither would sell."

Now, why didn't Wilma Wanderly want to tell me that? Quickly, the idea came to me that paying Bunny's sister for the dress was hardly flattering. And if she mentioned Bunny Hopper at all, it could have thrown a question over the rightful ownership of the dress she had. You really shouldn't buy a dress from someone other than the owner.

"Why did you tell her Jeffer had one of the dresses?"

"I didn't want to sell. If she thought she could get the dress elsewhere, she'd leave me alone. But, of course, she didn't."

Before we left, Louis took a couple of bills out of his wallet and offered them to Bunny. She didn't make a move, just continued to give us that icy stare.

"I hope it's not rude to offer a tip."

"Of course not," Bunny said. "It's customary to tip the dowager queen for an audience."

She waved her hand in the vague direction of her attendant, and he stepped forward and took the money. When he stepped back next to the Dowager Queen of Watts he slipped the money into her gloved hand.

That's when I realized Bunny Hopper was blind.

"How much did you give her, Louis?" Marc asked as we were driving home.

"Sixty."

"That's my sweet man," Marc said. "Poor Bunny. I can't

imagine being that sick and having to live off the kindness of my family."

"Especially when you end up paying for it anyway."

"Hopefully she's getting public assistance. There are programs that help you get medication if you're that poor."

"Hard to say. Blindness is an end-stage condition, though. She may not have been getting good care for a while."

I could barely breathe. There was too much about Bunny that reminded me of what had happened to Jeffer, and too much that told me what could happen to me.

"So, what next?" Marc asked.

"I don't know," I said, taking a deep calming breath. "I mean, now we know how Wilma got the dress she has. So it's definitely not the one stolen from Anthony."

"Unless she has both dresses," Louis said.

"But that's the point; to get two dresses. If she had both, why is she trying to get one from Noah?"

"Because they're not the right dresses," I said. "Maybe she's got two Dorothys, but what she wants is one Dorothy and one Wilma."

That made a lot of sense. I'd been just about to write Wilma off as a suspect, but that one idea put her back at the top of my list.

"So," Louis said. "Is there any way you do have a dress?"

"Yes and no."

"This ought to be interesting," he said to Marc.

Ignoring the comment, I said, "I dug through some old papers I have and found out that Jeffer had a secret bank account. One I didn't know about."

"It wouldn't be secret if you knew about it," Marc pointed out.

"Anyway, he was writing a check to cash for forty-nine dollars every month."

"That's an odd—oh, you think he was paying for a storage locker every month?"

"Yes, that's what I think."

"So who's been paying for it since he died?" Louis wanted to know.

Before I could answer, Marc said, "Oh my God. What happens if no one's paying for it?"

"I think they eventually auction off the contents sight unseen."

"So we might not ever know what happened to the dress?"

"We might not."

"I don't think Jeffer would let that happen," I said. "He really respected old Hollywood. He'd never let anything happen to the dress."

Of course, I felt a little foolish once I'd said that. He loved me and he'd let something terrible—"

"We should call around and see if we can find it," Marc said.

"I'm not even sure it's under his name, though," I said.

"Why do you think he hid this from you?"

"Louis, don't ask him that."

"Well, it is odd that he didn't tell Noah about the dress."

"No, it's not. There are all sorts of things I don't tell you."

"Do you have a secret storage compartment somewhere?"

"No. And I wouldn't tell you if I did."

"Now I want to know what kind of things you're not telling me."

"I'm not hiding anything important from you. And maybe that's the point. Jeffer didn't think the dress was that important."

"A man named Dick Congdon gave Jeffer the dress," I said. "They were together before Jeffer and me, or maybe even over-lapping. I'm not sure. That might have something to do with why he never said anything. It's certainly not the only secret Jeffer kept from me."

I blushed hard when I said the last part. Thankfully, neither of them asked about the other secrets Jeffer hid. We got back to our street and Louis jumped out to open the gate. Marc pulled into the carport.

It was eight thirty. I needed to get upstairs to have a little bite to eat and take my evening meds. We climbed up the red steps to the courtyard and I started to thank them for taking me, when I heard the phone ringing in my apartment.

I dashed up the steps to the second floor, pulling my keys out of my pocket as I ran. The answering machine had picked up as I inserted them in the door, and I could hear myself saying, "Hello. You've reached Noah. I'm not—"

Snatching up the phone, I said, "I'm here, I'm here."

"Noah? It's Carl."

"Hi Carl. Is something wrong?"

"Oh no, no, not really. I mean, I don't think so." Denny said something to him that I couldn't hear. Carl shushed him. "There's a gentleman here who'd like to speak to you. He's quite insistent."

"What's his name?"

"Lavender."

That stopped me. I didn't know anyone named Lavender. I think I'd remember if I did. Of course, I could have told Carl to say he should come back in the morning, but I knew I'd be too curious to sleep.

"Okay, I'll be right there."

Ten minutes later, I walked into Pinx and found a small man in a gray suit carrying a cane in a gloved hand, staring intently at the Hidden Treasures section. His suit, though high quality, looked as though it came from a vintage shop. His hair was very black and slicked back, and his skin was dangerously pale. He'd gone a long way to create the impression he'd just stepped out of a forties black-and-white film, and I was sure he'd take out a cigarette case and offer me one the minute I said hello.

"Are you Mr. Lavender?" I smirked to avoid outright laughter.

"Why yes, I am."

Instead of offering me a cigarette, he handed me his card. I read it. His name was more ridiculous than I thought.

"I don't mean to be rude, but Lance Lavender? That can't be your real name."

"Of course not, but Leopold Latislaw didn't look as good on the card."

I had news for him, Lance Lavender didn't look so hot either. The card also said he was a DEALER IN FINE COLLECTIBLES. "What can I do for you, Mr. Latislaw?"

He just smiled at my rudeness—but I wasn't going to call him Mr. Lavender. At least not without giggling.

"I'm here about the dress; the blue dress that was worn by Wilma Wanderly in *The Girl From Albany*."

"Who do you represent? Or are you here on your own?"

"I do have a client. A client who is willing to trade."

"Trade? What does your client want to trade?"

"A blue dress for a blue dress. My client has the dress worn by Dorothy Caine. He'd like the dress worn by Wilma Wanderly."

I had the very real sense he was telling me something. Something I'd almost but not quite figured out. Wilma had one of Dorothy's dresses and whoever killed Anthony Mercer had a dress, but I didn't know which one and I didn't know which one I might or might not have. Apparently, though, Lance Lavender did. And that could only mean one thing.

"Your client is a murderer."

"I don't have any reason to think that."

"You don't have any reason not to think it if this person has the dress that Anthony Mercer was killed for. We should at least be suspicious, don't you think?"

"If I listened to my suspicions I'd be out of business in a month. Are you willing to trade?"

"No, of course not. One blue dress is not like another."

"And if my client adds ten thousand dollars to sweeten the deal?"

"I don't actually have the dress, but if I did I would not trade you. You see, by trading with me you get a dress that you can explain. You got the dress from me. Which puts me in the awkward position of having a dress I can't explain."

"You could say that Jeffer had two dresses."

"But then there would be five dresses. The one Wilma

ruined, the one Dorothy sold and Wilma eventually bought, the one Anthony was killed for and the two that I got from Jeffer. You see, there's still a problem."

"I guess you have it all figured out, don't you?"

And I kind of thought I did. His client was Wilma, of course. I was sure of it. She'd paid one of her Mafia connections to kill Anthony only to find out he had Dorothy's dress. That left her with two dresses, but both were Dorothy's. Jeffer had a Wilma dress, somewhere. And now she was doing everything she could to get her hands on it.

"That's not all I've got figured out. Tell your client I know who they are and what they're up to."

"I think you're lying."

"But it's not up to you, is it? It's up to your client."

10

I SLEPT POORLY THAT NIGHT. I HAD WEIRD DREAMS ABOUT being back in my house with Jeffer. He'd rearranged our furniture and I was furious that he hadn't at least talked to me before doing it. Not knowing where things were left me stumbling around the house stubbing my toes.

The dream woke me, and I stayed awake for a few hours, tossing and turning. The meaning of the dream was so obvious: Jeffer had lied to me, and that had rearranged my life completely leaving me out of all the decisions. And yes, it did make me angry. My toes, however, were just fine.

When I got up the next morning, Louis was down in the courtyard yelling, "Marc! Marc!"

Groggy and exhausted, I sat up in bed listening to what was happening. A moment later, I heard Marc come out of their apartment and say, "Oh, my."

Something had happened. I got out of bed, pulled on a pair of cut-offs and a T-shirt, and put on my *Minty* baseball cap. I lumbered into the bathroom and brushed my teeth. I took two steps out my door and looked down at the courtyard. Splayed across the iron table where we'd had so many meals was the corpse of a young man nearing thirty. I had a bad case of déjà vu. And unfortunately it wasn't one of the side effects of AZT. It was actual, real, déjà vu.

Louis looked up at me and asked, "Anyone you know?"

"I've never seen him before in my life."

I could hear Marc inside calling the police. I really hoped I'd had nothing to do with the corpse, a pretty vain hope since I was pretty sure the corpse would turn out to have something to do with me. Or at least with the blue dress I supposedly had—if I could figure out where it was.

I went downstairs and joined Louis. There was little to do but stand there and stare at the corpse. It looked as though he'd been a very attractive young man. He had a well-proportioned face, square jaw, and eyes that would be very pretty if they hadn't already turned opaque. He lay face up and I couldn't see what had killed him, though I suspected there was a bullet hole in the back of his head.

I doubted he was killed in the courtyard, which meant someone went to the trouble of driving him here, and then climbing the red steps with the corpse slung over their shoulder. The idea that we were looking for someone very large crossed my mind.

Whoever the corpse had been, he hadn't dressed for going anyplace special. He wore a pair of jeans and a UCLA sweatshirt with a hood. The sweatshirt looked warm, which suggested he'd gone out late. The weather recently had been low seventies in the morning but warmer in the afternoon, sometimes well into the eighties. At night the temperature dipped into the low sixties. He was dressed for night.

Marc came out and stood next to us.

"Should we really stand here gawking at him?" he asked.

Louis, who was on the opposite side of the table, looked at me and said, "This is becoming a pattern with you, isn't it?"

I'd had the misfortune of having a corpse dropped in my vicinity before.

"Me? I'd say this one is on you two. He's closer to you guys than he is to me."

"The killer probably just got tired and couldn't face another flight of stairs."

"Louis, you're going to give him a complex. Stop it."

A siren started in the distance and grew closer.

"Nobody heard anything?" Louis asked.

Marc and I shook our heads.

"Oh, wait. I was awake from around two to four. I didn't hear anything, but I would have. This must have happened either before or after."

"What time did you go to sleep?"

"I think by ten."

"We were up until nearly midnight," Marc said.

"So the body was dumped here between midnight and two a.m., or four and six," Louis calculated.

"Why six," I asked.

"Sunrise. Nobody wants the sun coming up on them while they're carrying a dead body."

The siren was on top of us and we heard a car pull up, doors opening, radios chattering. A minute or two later, a uniformed officer came up the steps. He was a decent looking guy about my age. It took him only a moment to see the problem on our patio table. He immediately spoke into a radio device on his shoulder.

Then he said to us, "I'm going to need you to back away from the body. I have to create a perimeter."

We stepped back, but not far enough. When it became clear that the perimeter was probably going to cover their front door, I said to Marc and Louis, "Come on. Let's go upstairs."

I brought out my dining chairs and set them in front of my living room window on the narrow walkway that ran the length of my apartment. From there, Marc, Louis and I had an excellent view of everything the police where doing.

Louis didn't sit though. Instead, he said, "I'll make coffee," and disappeared into my apartment.

Both Marc and Louis were partly dressed for work.

"You should call your office and tell them you're not coming in," Louis said.

"This is going to cause a dilemma," Marc replied, staring over the railing at the body downstairs.

"How so?"

"Is this a sick day, a vacation day or a floating holiday? I know I should get the day off for discovering a dead body outside my door, I just don't know what kind of day to call it."

He was only half serious, so I said, "You're right, the studios should have thought ahead. I think it's a personal day."

"That'll work. Can I use your phone?"

I nodded and went inside. I was alone for a moment on the balcony. Detective O'Shea came up the steps, along with another detective—a woman, who looked confused and angry, and only more so when she saw the corpse. O'Shea looked at the corpse and then up at me. I gave him a little nod. He gave me a half smile in return.

A few minutes later, Marc and Louis had both called their offices and canceled work for the day, then they came out and sat down. Louis handed out cups of coffee. To Marc he said, "We need to buy Noah a coffee grinder and some decent beans."

"I doubt this is going to become a frequent occurrence," I said hopefully.

"That's no reason not to be prepared." Then Louis said, as though I might not be aware, "You have no food. No milk, no eggs, no flour. There's nothing in there for me to make us breakfast."

"I can make toast."

"You don't have any jam."

I used to cook. When I was with Jeffer. I was a good cook. I cooked for the two us. I cooked for company. In fact, I made dinner for Anthony Mercer. Something with pork and apples, I think. What I didn't do was cook for myself. Cooking for one was just messy and time consuming and depressing.

Detective O'Shea looked through the corpse's pockets. He reached underneath him and pulled out a wallet, opened it up and took out a license. Then he went over to his partner and said a few things. I wanted to ask who the victim was, but decided I ought to try being patient.

"Let's have this one cup of coffee, then we'll go down to Millie's," Marc suggested.

"That's not a bad idea," Louis said. "If they let us leave."

"We'll come back. We live here. Plus we know Detective O'Shea. He knows we'll come back."

"Tall, Dark and Menacing," Louis said. It was what he'd called O'Shea before we knew he was a pretty good guy.

"You can't call him that anymore," I said. "He's a nice guy."

"Tall, Dark and Amazing?" Louis said and winked at me. I couldn't help blushing.

Two men from the coroner's office arrived in their dark blue windbreakers. They'd be taking those jackets off in an hour or two. They started poking around the body, and making comments to O'Shea and his partner.

I took a sip of my coffee. It was hot and rich. Louis hated that I used coffee in a can, but really he managed to make it taste good. Better than when I made it for myself.

"We are going to have to wipe that table down with bleach, aren't we?" Marc said. "Multiple times."

"Now, now, he was shot. He didn't die of the bubonic plague."

"Louis. Watch what you say. I'll make you throw the table away and buy a new one."

"We'll bleach the table. That's fine. But let's not go overboard."

"You could use a table cloth," I suggested. "The kind that's coated in plastic."

O'Shea's partner was pointing at us, asking him something. Presumably, if she should come up and talk to us. He looked up and nearly smirked. Then he nodded his head at her.

She climbed up the stairs. Medium height, she wore a simple pair of brown polyester slacks, brown shoes, and a dress shirt she might have gotten in the boy's department. Her long brown hair was barely combed no less styled, her eyes squinted behind a pair of ill-fitting glasses, and what make-up she wore was misapplied.

I knew exactly what Jeffer would have said the first time he saw her. He'd have said she obviously didn't have any gay friends. I wondered, though, if it wasn't all a bit deliberate. She took out a small, spiral notebook and a pen, opened the notebook and took notes as she listened.

"I'm Detective Brenda Wellesley. Which one of you found the body?"

"I did," Louis said.

"And which apartment are you in?"

"1A, directly below."

"And this apartment is?"

"2A," I said.

She pushed her glasses back up her nose. "You live downstairs and you live upstairs. Where do you live?" she asked, pointing at Marc.

"I live downstairs."

"Next door, in 1B?"

"No. In 1A with Louis."

That earned him an unpleasant stare.

"Do you want our names?" Marc asked. "It might make this easier."

She ignored him. Instead, she asked Louis, "Tell me what happened?"

"I was getting ready for work. I was walking through the living room on my way to make coffee in the kitchen, when I noticed that that table didn't look right. I came out to see what was wrong, and there was that guy just laying there."

"And what did you do then?"

"I screamed for Marc."

She looked at me and said, "You're Marc."

"I'm Noah."

"I'm Marc."

"So you came out after this gentleman called for you?"

"Louis. His name is Louis. And, yes."

"And what about you?" she asked me. "When did you come out?"

"Around the same time. I heard them talking and I knew something was wrong."

"So which one of you touched the body?"

"I don't think any of us touched the body," Louis said.

"Then how did you know he was dead?" She asked.

"He looked dead."

"He looked very dead," Marc added in support.

"You're familiar with dead people?"

"No," Marc admitted.

"His eyes were clouded over though," Louis said. "I think that means he died at least a few hours before."

"Why do you think that?"

"I don't know. I probably saw something about it on TV."

"No you didn't," she said, though he really could have.

Louis stared at her then said, "A friend of mine died. I was allowed to say my goodbyes. His eyes were like that. The nurse said it happens a couple of hours after someone dies."

She studied him for a moment. Then she looked at me, pushing her glasses up her nose again as she did. "Did you hear anything during the night?"

"No, but this is interesting. You see we figured something out: The body was brought here either between midnight and two or between four and six."

"Don't do that."

"Do what?"

"Figure things out. So you didn't hear anything?"

"No. I went to bed at—"

She raised her hand to stop me from speaking and asked Louis, "And you didn't hear anything?"

"No."

"And neither did you?" she said to Marc.

"No, I didn't hear anything."

She turned back to Louis and asked, "How well did you know him?"

"The dead guy? I didn't. I've never met him in my life."

"We're going to find out. You'll save us some time if you just admit you knew him."

"But I didn't know him."

She turned to Marc and said, "What about you? You knew him, didn't you?"

Marc rolled his eyes. "No. I did *not* know him."

Squinting her eyes at Marc, she made a few marks in the notebook. The she moved on to me.

"What about you? Did you know him?"

"Not exactly," I said.

"What is that supposed to mean?"

"It means, I think his first name might be Brick."

"And why do you think that?"

"We heard that Anthony Mercer had a date with someone named Brick on the night he died."

"Anthony Mercer," she said, squinting her eyes. Then she leaned over the railing, asking, "Javier, is this a joke?"

He raised his hands the air and shrugged.

"All right, who is we?"

"Us," Louis said.

"The three of you?"

We nodded. It didn't seem like such a great idea to bring Leon into this right now.

"And how did you find out about this date?"

"At brunch."

"It was sort of a memorial for Anthony," Louis explained.

"You were friends with Mercer?"

We shook our heads.

"Why did you go to a memorial for someone you weren't friends with?"

"We didn't go to it. We gave it,"' Louis said.

"We were investigating the murder," Marc added.

"Really? A murder that's none of your business?"

"It is kind of Noah's business."

She turned on me. "And why is it your business?"

"Well, because Wilma Wanderly thinks I have a blue sequined dress."

After taking three slow, controlled breaths she screamed, "JAVIER!"

Millie's was a small café on Sunset right at the bottom of our hill. Operating out of a small storefront for sixty-some years, the place sat about twenty-five people, not including a couple of tables it kept (illegally, I think) on the sidewalk. It was nearly impossible to get a table on the weekend, but on a Thursday morning we didn't have much trouble.

The deep purple walls were covered in memorabilia from the forties: vintage Coca Cola trays and cigarette ads, hard plastic Kewpie dolls and saddle shoes. The three of us sat at a tiny table for four. The waitress, whose jeans were ripped across both knees and had her hair dyed black and cut like Betty Page, seemed more interested in snapping her gum than taking our order. Still, we persevered.

Louis ordered chilaquiles, Marc had huevos rancheros, I ordered a single pancake with an egg over easy. We all asked for coffee. Before the waitress walked away, Louis ordered me a vanilla shake to go with my breakfast.

"Please, don't order for me," I said.

"A pancake and an egg is not enough food."

I wasn't entirely sure I'd be able to finish the pancake.

"Louis, he's a grown-up person," Marc said. "Let him make his own decisions."

The waitress was already back with our coffees. She passed them around and said, "Your milkshake will be up in a minute."

"So," Louis said as soon as she walked away. "What do we think of this morning's events?"

"I think Detective Wellesley needs to work on her social skills," I said.

"Obviously," Marc agreed.

"Two questions. Why kill Brick, if that was indeed Brick? And why now?"

"Oh crap," I said.

"What?"

"I think it's my fault."

"You killed him and carried him up the stairs?" Marc guessed.

"No, after we came back from Watts I got a call from Pinx. There was a man there looking for me. A collector calling himself Lance Lavender."

"That can't be his real name."

"No. His real name is Leopold Latislaw."

"That's not any better," Marc said. "Why is no one named Bob anymore? Or Willy? Or Tom?"

"Are you saying too many people are named Marc?" Louis teased.

"Oh my God, every other person is named Marc."

Shaking my head, I continued, "Lavender said he had a client who'd trade dresses with me. Apparently, the dress that was stolen from Anthony was Dorothy's back up dress."

"So his client must be Wilma Wanderly," Marc said.

"That's what I thought. So I told him I knew who his client was, and what they were up to."

"And a corpse shows up in our courtyard a few hours later," Louis said.

"Yes," I said, cringing.

"Someone's trying to send a message."

"But *is* it Wilma Wanderly?" Marc asked. "She certainly didn't throw that guy over her shoulder and carry him up the stairs."

"Obviously, she hired someone."

"From the parking lot at Home Depot?"

"Louis. Don't be racist."

"Well, where does a movie star hire help for committing a crime?" I asked, tongue in cheek.

"Central casting," joked Marc.

"I imagine her son is helping her," Louis suggested, more realistically.

"Possibly," I said. "But he seems very, I don't know, inept. And she's browbeaten the life out of him."

"So he'd do whatever she asked of him."

"Yes, but I doubt he'd do it to her satisfaction. It's hard to imagine him killing someone and then delivering the corpse to our courtyard without making a half-dozen mistakes. Plus, he's like, fifty. I don't know if he could throw a corpse over his shoulder and climb a flight of stairs."

The waitress arrived with my milkshake. I stuck the straw in and took a long sip. It was wonderful. And then it wasn't. It started off sweet and full of the taste of vanilla, but then it turned chalky and fatty. I swallowed it anyway.

Before I left the house, I'd wrapped my pills in a tissue. I pulled the wad out of my pocket and, under the table, unrolled the wad. Popping them quickly into my mouth, I chased them with another good long draft of the milkshake. Hopefully, my last. Then I looked at Marc and Louis and said, "Vitamins."

"Just to play devil's advocate," Marc began. "What if it's not Wilma Wanderly? Who else could it be?"

"Dorothy Caine," Louis suggested.

"Like Wilma, she'd need a lot of help."

"Bunny Hopper. She has minions. We saw one of them. And she wants her dress back."

"She wants *her* dress back. Wilma has her dress. I think she'd kill Wilma before she'd kill Anthony."

"What if Lance Lavender doesn't have a client?" I suggested. "What if he were trying to get the dress for himself?"

"Then why trade? Why not just buy the dress?"

"Maybe trading was just a way to maneuver me into the right place so he could kill me and steal the dress just like he did with Anthony."

"May have," Marc corrected. "Lavender may have killed Anthony. And, it doesn't explain the corpse in our courtyard. If Lavender is the one collecting dresses he doesn't have a reason to leave the corpse there. No, I'm still wondering about Hollywood Costume. What if the blue dresses are just a way to shield the real crime? That the guy who owns Hollywood Costume killed Mercer so he could take over his business."

"Do we know anyone who works there or knows a lot about them?" Louis asked.

"I do. My former friend Robert works there."

Our breakfasts arrived and so did Detective O'Shea. The waitress asked if he wanted anything and he ordered a couple of eggs with bacon. When the waitress was gone, he asked, "So, have the three of you solved the crime?"

"Crime*s*," Marc corrected.

"So you think this is connected to Anthony Mercer's death?"

"Isn't it?" I asked.

"The man in the courtyard is named Brick Leland Masters. So, yes, I'd say they were connected. Does that name ring any bells for you?"

"Just the Brick part," I said.

"His address is in the Hollywood flats. We'll go search his apartment later today."

"How was he killed?" I asked.

"It appears he was shot in the back of the head like Anthony Mercer."

"You're looking for someone large," I said. "They obviously carried the corpse over their shoulder up the stairs."

"That's a good guess," O'Shea said. "But we've already seen some post-mortem bruising and will likely discover more when the coroner removes all his clothing. It looks as though he was dragged up the stairs. Blood stains and scuffing on the stairs seem to support that conclusion."

"Oh, okay."

He smiled at me. "Yours was a good guess, though."

"Do you know anything else about Brick Masters?" Louis asked.

"There was a SAG card in his wallet."

"A wannabe actor moonlighting as a hit man, now I've heard everything," Marc moaned.

Our breakfasts arrived and I told O'Shea all about Dorothy Caine, Bunny Hopper and Lance Lavender. I wanted to keep O'Shea up to date, and I also wanted to avoid my breakfast. I was pretty full from the milkshake. O'Shea stopped me, saying, "Eat your breakfast. You can catch me up later."

I took a tiny bite of pancake and said, "Do you think Brick was dumped in my courtyard to make me look guilty?"

"No. The killer is trying to frighten you."

"Well, it's working."

"You don't think Brick was killed specifically to scare Noah, do you?" Louis asked.

"No. Brick knew too much. The killer was killing two birds with one stone."

"Oh great," Marc said. "A bird killer."

11

Marc and Louis had tickets for *Tamara* that evening at the American Legion Hall on Highland. They'd been before, several times actually. The play was about an Italian painter, but it was performed in different rooms of the "villa" and the audience chose which characters to follow or not follow. They'd talked about it several times and I gathered they still didn't know what it was all about.

I'd spent the afternoon at Pinx poking around at things I was supposed to be doing but accomplishing little. I didn't bring home a video—there wasn't anything I really wanted to see—besides, I liked TV on Wednesday night. My plan was to force down an entire Budget Gourmet and watch *Beverly Hills, 90210* and *Melrose Place*—despite the fact that my reception would not be good. Both shows confirmed something I'd long believed: Heterosexuals were manipulative, conniving schemers, who did nothing but ruin one another's lives. The shows were the very definition of guilty pleasure.

But when I walked into my apartment and threw my keys into the dish on the top of my bookcase, I noticed the blue-inked business card Wilma Wanderly had given me. Glancing at my watch, I noted it was seven thirty. If I hurried I could go see her and be back in time for *Melrose Place*. Unless, of course, she killed me. But she couldn't kill me. Not until she had the dress she thought I had. So I was safe—for now.

The Wanderly Estate was in Nicholas Canyon and modest by Hollywood standards. It sat behind a stucco wall and an electronic gate. There was barely enough room between the street and the gate to accommodate my very small car. I pressed the call button.

Albert came on, "Yes?"

"It's Noah Valentine here to see Miss Wanderly."

He didn't answer. He just hit whatever button opened the gate. The front yard was little more than a concrete parking lot, with Wilma's limo sitting in front of the house (apparently too large for the garage). The front of the house had a double door and a couple of small windows, making the house seem small. But the roof was oversized to accommodate a hidden second floor. My guess was the windows were in the back and opened onto the canyon.

I parked in front of the garage and walked over to the door. I rang the bell and waited. Finally, Wilma Wanderly opened the double door, pulling both doors open dramatically, and stood there wearing a filmy apricot affair that was half dress/half negligee, and a perfectly styled lemony wig. Without inviting me in, she turned and crossed the foyer to the living room. I shut the front doors behind me and followed.

The living room was down a step and large enough to comfortably hold two large sofas with a wide marble coffee table between them. On the far side of the room was a grand piano. As I'd suspected, one wall of the living room was glass and looked out on a pool lit from below.

"Anthony is bringing down my dinner in a few minutes. I hope you don't mind. He lives in the house out back."

I hoped it was an actual house and not another oversized doghouse. I smiled at her and said, "I don't mind."

"Having a child who's endlessly devoted to you is more burdensome than it might seem."

"Is it?"

"Of course, it would have been easier if there were something interesting about him. I mean, if I have to have a gay son, why couldn't he be an interesting gay, like a decorator or a makeup artist or costumer. A costumer would have been ideal, I'd have saved so much money."

"I didn't think, I didn't know...." I tried to say.

"Well, yes, he refuses to come out. I mean, he's a middle-aged man who's not married, of course he's gay. He even pretended to be in love with this ridiculously tall girl once just to keep me in the dark. But I knew; and I made sure that poor girl knew."

I was about to ask her a more relevant question when Albert walked in carrying a tray. In the light, he was an unattractive, middle-aged man with a weak jaw and dark, prominent lips.

He set the tray down on the coffee table. On it was a bowl of soup and a grilled sandwich. She immediately reached out and dipped a well-manicured finger into the soup. Putting her soup-covered finger into her mouth, she gave Albert a disappointed look.

"The soup needs to be scalding. How many times have I told you that? It cools off too fast as you come across the yard."

"I'll warm it up in the microwave."

"No. I don't want radiation on my food. Take it back."

"Why don't I use the kitchen down here?"

"And make a mess for Manuela? No. Take it back and try again." Albert bent over and reached for the tray. Before he could take the tray back she snatched the sandwich off its plate and kept it.

"Mother, wouldn't it be better if I got you your soup later?"

"Oh, no, I'm fine. I'm sure Mr. Valentine has good news for me. There's nothing to worry about."

Albert looked at me for confirmation. I didn't want to lie, but I also wanted him to go away. I just smiled at him, hoping it was a friendly smile. Clearly unhappy, Albert walked out of the room. A moment later there was a loud crash when he dropped the soup.

Wilma took the Lord's name in vain.

"So, you're here to sell me the dress, aren't you?" She took a delicate bite of her sandwich.

"Not exactly."

"What does that mean? Not exactly?"

"Jeffer had a storage facility somewhere that he was paying for, but I don't know where."

"Well, have you called around?"

"No. Jeffer paid in cash. I doubt it's under his name."

"I'm not sure I believe you. He was your friend, why was he so secretive?"

I nearly said, "Habit," but that would have been bitter. And bitter wouldn't get my questions answered. "Jeffer wasn't always forthcoming. I don't know why he kept the dress a secret. I'm trying to figure that out myself."

"Maybe you're not the trustworthy sort. Have you considered that?"

"I've considered everything." I said stiffly. Then I turned the tables on her, "You went to see Anthony Mercer, didn't you?"

"Yes, of course I did. He had something I wanted."

"But he wouldn't sell it to you, do you know why?"

"Where did you get an idea like that? He was going to sell me the dress. We hadn't worked out all the details, but he'd agreed. I was paying him twenty-five thousand dollars. We'd been negotiating for almost two months and were ready to sign the contract. Then he was killed and the dress is…well, who knows where the dress is."

I was stunned. This changed everything. If Anthony Mercer really was going to sell Wilma the dress there was no reason for her to kill him. So, if she didn't do it, who did?

"Do you want to see it?"

"See what?"

"The dress."

"Oh. Yes, of course."

She lay the sandwich down on the coffee table. She'd only taken a few bites. And then she floated out of the room. I followed her. We climbed the stairs to the second floor and entered the master bedroom, which was directly above the living room. It, too, had a wall of windows though they were covered in heavily lined satin drapes. Wilma went immediately to a closet, one of many, and threw open the doors. She reached in and pulled out the dress. It caught the light and shimmered. The blue of the sequins was so intense they nearly glowed.

Wilma had to hold the dress above her shoulder. It was clearly too big for her. Even from where I was standing I could see that someone had sewn a label in the back of the dress that said, DOROTHY CAINE.

"You got this from Bunny Hopper?"

"Yes, I did. I think he tried to wear it himself. It's a little stretched out in places." That was hardly fair. Bunny wasn't much bigger than Wilma and certainly too small for the dress.

"So, Anthony had your backup dress?" I said, even though I thought I knew the answer.

"No. He had Dorothy's backup dress."

"But you still wanted it? You were still paying twenty-five thousand for it?"

"Of course. You put two of the dresses together in a display and no one's going to measure them."

"A display?"

"I'm returning to Las Vegas. Lucky Days Casino. They're renovating the Kismet Room just for me. I'm going to have the dresses put into a plexiglass case so the audience can see them as they come in. So you see why it's important you find a second dress?"

I was a tad speechless. She was too old and too frail to head-line a Vegas review. What was she thinking?

"Did he have dementia at the end?" Wilma asked. "I've heard that happens to some of the boys."

"What? Who?"

"Jeffer. That might explain the secrecy."

"No! No! Really? I don't believe it," Leon was completely flummoxed. "There was a dead body right here on this table. And not one of you thought to call me?"

The four of us sat around the table after our weekly dinner. Tiki torches were lit at the edge of the courtyard and there were cream-colored IKEA candles on the table. The boom box sitting outside Marc and Louis' apartment played Chet Baker.

For dinner, Louis had made a casserole of beef, spinach, cheese and quinoa. It was tasty and I'd actually eaten a lot of what Louis had put on my plate.

Leon, though, had complained, "What on Earth is keen-wha? Or should I say keen-what?"

"It's a grain, like rice," Louis explained. "Lots of iron."

That made me blush. The quinoa was my fault. It wasn't bad, but it also wasn't pasta. Leon frowned. "I suspect there's a lot of iron in beef stroganoff as well."

"Not as much. I checked."

"You really didn't have to, Louis," I said.

"Oh, yes he did," Marc said. "You know how he is. If we didn't have you we'd have an apartment full of stray animals. You're at least housebroken."

I blushed again.

"Marc," Louis said, softly.

"It was a joke." To me he added, "I don't really think you're a stray animal."

But I think he did. And for that matter so did I. It was an uncomfortable moment; one I covered by bringing up a dead body. I turned to Leon and said, "Actually, if the body was still here, his head would be right in your lap."

"I wish I could say it was the first time I've had a lifeless head in my lap, but it's not," Leon said, emptying his wine glass. Louis refilled it.

"Have you talked to Tall, Dark and Delicious since yester-day?" Louis asked. "Has he made any progress on the case?"

"No, I haven't talked to him," I said.

"I keep expecting to hear that they've arrested Wilma Wanderly," Marc said, exhaling a long plume of smoke. "Can you imagine what that's going to be like? The press is going to go insane: Faded Star Kills for Tattered Dress."

"She didn't, though," I said. "And the dress isn't tattered."

They all turned to look at me.

"What?"

"Huh?"

"Excuse me?"

"Wilma Wanderly didn't kill Anthony Mercer. Or Brick Masters. Anthony was going to sell her the dress for twenty-five thousand, so she had no reason to kill him. In fact, when he died she lost the dress."

"How did you find that out?" Leon asked.

"I went to see her."

"She could be lying," Louis speculated.

"I don't think so. She wants two dresses because she's planning a Vegas comeback."

"She's not going to wear them?" Marc said, somewhat aghast.

"Not this time, no. She wants to put them in the lobby of the theater. In a display case."

"She's willing to pay twenty-five thousand dollars just to put a couple of dresses in the lobby?" Louis asked.

"Thirty," I said. "She paid five for the first dress."

"She can get a lot of publicity from the dresses," Marc explained. "Publicity worth far more than thirty-thousand dollars."

Then all three boys were looking behind me, so I turned around and there, standing roughly in the spot where I'd fainted, was my former friend Tina. She wore cowboy boots, one of her long, baggy dresses with a small jean jacket over it, and carried a large purse made from an old quilt. She wore her hair piled loosely on her head with a giant tortoise shell clip holding it together.

I said, "Excuse me a minute," to the table and walked over to her.

"I'm glad to see you're all right," she said when I got close.

"I'm fine. What are you doing here?"

"I've been thinking about everything, a lot, and I think I owe you an apology."

"It doesn't matter."

"But it does matter, Noah. It matters a lot. I kept trying to understand why you didn't say anything and then I realized the awful thing I did to you, the worst thing I did, was not trusting you. I should have stayed out of things with Jeffer. I should have trusted that you had good reasons for the things you did. And that's what I should do now. I'm just going to trust you. You don't have to explain anything. You just have to accept my apology."

She brushed a tear from her eye, making a mess of the bit of mascara she wore, and ruining any possibility of my rejecting the apology.

"I'm just so angry at Jeffer," she said.

"That's why I didn't tell you. He was so afraid of dying alone."

And then Louis was there, handing Tina a glass of wine and saying, "You're in time for dessert."

"Oh, thank you. I just stopped by for a moment, though."

"From the Westside?" Louis said, remembering something I'd said weeks before.

"It's more West Hollywood than the Westside," she said. West Hollywood was more center city and definitely not dripping in money like Beverly Hills, Holmby Hills or the Palisades —the real Westside. "I should get going. I have two scripts to read before tomorrow."

"One glass of wine," Louis coaxed. "And a tiny piece of cake."

"You have to try Louis' cake." I said, as a way to tell her she could stay.

She smiled. "Well, maybe just a few minutes."

Someone had already added a chair to the table, and we went back over and sat down.

"Did you meet everyone at the memorial?" I asked.

"I didn't meet anyone at the memorial," she said. "You

passed out right after I got there and then the whole thing was over."

"Party pooper," Leon called me.

I introduced everyone. Then Louis walked into the apartment to get dessert.

"Did you know Anthony Mercer?" Leon asked.

"No. My friend Robert knew him through work."

"Robert works at Hollywood Costume," I explained.

"Does he now," Leon said. "Has he mentioned anything about them buying out Mercy Costumes?"

"Not exactly. Something's going on, though," she said. "Robert's been very secretive lately."

"We've been trying to figure out who killed Anthony," Marc explained.

"Seriously?" she asked. Then looked around the table like it was a joke she wasn't in on.

"It wasn't Wilma Wanderly," I said.

"But it might have been Billy Martinez," said Leon.

"Wait. That's Robert's boss," Tina said, lighting a cigarette. "Billy wouldn't kill anyone."

"Would he hire a killer, though?"

She looked at us for a moment then said, "I don't know. Robert says he's ruthless, but I didn't think that means…"

"What about Robert's relationship with his boss? What's that like?" I asked.

"It's contentious. They fight. Robert's come home several times convinced he was going to get fired. But I think that's just Billy's artistic temperament."

Louis came out carrying a three-layer chocolate cake with a lit sparkler on top. I glanced around. Whose birthday had I forgotten? Marc's? Leon's? Then Louis set the cake down in front of me.

"Guys! Guys! It's not my birthday."

"No, it's not," said Louis. "It is the one year anniversary of your moving in, though."

My lease was month-to-month so I hadn't had to renew, which might have reminded me. I wouldn't have appreciated it though. I hated thinking about the anniversary. Jeffer died a couple of weeks after I moved in and then the mess with his family went on for months.

Louis took the sparkler out of the cake and began to cut it up.

"He was very mysterious at first," Marc said to Tina. "It took us almost six months to get him to come to dinner. And then when he did come he barely said a word."

"Do you guys take turns cooking?" she asked.

That drew a hearty laugh.

"Oh my dear," said Leon. "I couldn't find a kitchen with a map."

"Louis does the cooking," Marc said. "The rest of us are hopeless."

"That's not true," Tina said. "Noah is an excellent cook. He and Jeffer entertained all the time. But Noah did everything."

"Why did you keep this a secret?" Louis asked, handing out cake.

"I didn't keep it a secret. I'm pretty sure I mentioned that Anthony Mercer came to dinner."

"Yes, but we assumed Jeffer was the one who cooked," Marc said.

"Jeffer!" Tina laughed. "Jeffer was far too creative to follow a recipe."

"Well, you'll have to cook for us sometime," Leon said, digging into his cake.

"Here's a random thought," Louis said, abruptly. "Who inherits Mercy Costumes?"

We all stared blankly at one another. We had no idea.

12

It was my job to call Tall, Dark and—I mean, Detective O'Shea. After dinner we'd come up with a short list of steps we could take toward finding Anthony's killer. I got, 'Ask O'Shea about the will.' I wasn't sure he'd give me that kind of information, but I said I'd try.

Louis had an idea about running a credit check on Anthony to see what his financial picture was like. He might have been having financial difficulties, which would explain why he was selling the dress. Louis would make lemon bars laced with Cointreau to take down to the collections department to see if he couldn't coax someone into running a credit report.

Leon promised to call a couple of Anthony's friends who were at the memorial brunch to see if they knew anything about Brick Masters. Specifically, did Billy Martinez know Brick Masters.

"Oh my God," Leon said when he got his assignment. "They have the same initials. I wonder if that's an omen."

"If by omen you mean a coincidence, yes," replied Marc.

Marc was going to call SAG and see if Brick Masters had an agent. And if he didn't have an agent, he'd try to find out his address.

Tina, who really shouldn't have taken an assignment, offered to talk to Robert about whether Hollywood Costume really was buying Mercy Costumes and if so how the deal was progressing.

We promised to meet up at New York, New York for happy hour.

The next morning, I got up around nine. I called Rampart Station and got Detective O'Shea on the phone. I was ready to ask my questions over the phone, but he suggested we have coffee. I agreed to meet him in half an hour. I took a quick shower and threw on a pair of jean shorts, a striped Gap T-shirt, a work shirt and a pair of white Reebok high-tops. My hair was hopeless, so I grabbed the *Minty* cap that Marc had given me, thinking I should probably ask him to get me a cap for a show that was still on the air.

We met at The Living Room, a coffeehouse on Sunset across from the Mercado where Louis loved to shop. Occupying a storefront not unlike Pinx, The Living Room had recently taken over for a failed health food store. They'd gutted the inside, polished the concrete, put down a couple of threadbare Persian rugs, found a collection of mismatched living room furniture from the fifties and sixties, lined the sides with bookcases, and hung a blackboard menu from the ceiling. Then they opened.

It was a very popular place, half gay/half straight, the kind of place where you were very comfortable if you'd managed to shed your Midwestern narrow-mindedness. If you hadn't you'd be better off driving down to Orange County for coffee.

I got a French roast and a banana muffin. Then I found a leather wingback chair across from a French provincial occasional chair with a small café table between them. I sipped my coffee and took a few tentative bites of the muffin. My stomach seemed okay. Maybe it was even improving.

For a bit, I watched for O'Shea, but got bored and began studying the bookshelves behind me. The books seemed to be bestsellers from the sixties and seventies. I'm not a big reader, but I did recognize the titles of the ones that had been made into movies. And there were several of those. *The Godfather* by Mario Puzo, *Looking for Mr. Goodbar* by Judith Rossner, and *Jaws* by Peter Benchley—which I'd had no idea was ever a book.

"Why didn't you get a fancy coffee?" Detective O'Shea asked as he sat down. The coffee he held in one hand looked like it might be a cappuccino. He dropped a sugar cube into it and stirred.

"I'm fine with regular coffee."

"I'm glad you called me," he said.

I smiled. I decided I'd better offer him some information before asking questions. He'd be more likely to share with me if I shared with him.

"I talked to Wilma Wanderly. She doesn't have a motive. In fact, Anthony's murder screwed up a deal she was making with him."

"Yes, I know all that."

"Oh, okay." I smiled uncomfortably. "So, we were wondering if you knew who gets Anthony's business."

"I can't give you that information."

"But, you told us things about the way Anthony was shot."

"That was all in the newspaper. You might think about a subscription."

"Billy Martinez, the owner of Hollywood Costume, wants to buy Anthony's business. But we've heard that Anthony didn't want to sell. So we thought whoever—"

"Yes, I see where you're going with this. No offense, but I'm way ahead of you. It's my job after all."

"Well, give me a hint at least. Are we barking up the wrong tree?"

"Are you going to the parade on Sunday?"

"Yeah, a bunch of us are."

"I've never done that." He fidgeted in his chair.

"Oh, well, it's generally too hot, too long, too crowded and too boring," I shrugged. "But it's an important thing to do."

He smiled and looked away. Something about my answer had been disappointing. "So you're not originally from L.A., are you?"

"No, I'm from the Midwest."

"Where in the Midwest?"

"Michigan. Grand Rapids."

"What was that like?"

"Cold. Underpopulated. Boring."

"Sounds charming," he said. "You either think everything is boring or you don't want to talk to me."

"I want to talk to you," I said. "I called you, remember?"

"But you only want to talk about my case."

He was right, of course. He'd asked me where I grew up and what it was like. I was supposed to do the same but didn't. I didn't because then this would become a date. A coffee date.

Crap, he'd tricked me. Well, I wasn't going to stand for it. I asked another question about his case. "So you think Wilma Wanderly is telling the truth about her deal with Anthony?"

He sighed and shook his head. "Yes, I do. Anthony told people he was going to sell the dress to Miss Wanderly."

"He did? Who? Did he need money?"

"Don't try to make anything out of that. And leave Miss Wanderly alone, okay?"

"Um, sure, okay."

Detective O'Shea leaned back in his chair and looked at me intently. Very intently. "See, here's the thing. I think you like me. I think that's why you're sticking your nose into something that's really not your business."

"But, the dress—"

"Probably doesn't have anything to do with Anthony's murder. Isn't that what you were just telling me?"

"Yes, I suppose."

"So there wasn't really any reason at all to call me this morning. Was there?"

I could have told him that I'd promised my friends I'd call and find out about the will—except, he was right. I could have said no. I could have said I didn't want anything to do with figuring out Anthony's murder. In fact, that had been my first impulse.

When I didn't say anything, he stood up and walked out of the coffeehouse. I sipped my coffee. It was ice cold. I tried to decide if I wanted a refill.

O'Shea was wrong that I was only doing this because I liked

him. I had tried not to be involved. It wasn't my fault people kept showing up on my doorstep, dead and alive. Besides, I knew Anthony, kind of. My friends and I might actually be able to help track down his killer. People would say things to us they wouldn't say to Detective O'Shea.

Or maybe I *was* doing this because I liked him.

Just a little.

I did order another coffee, to go. Then I drove over to Hyperion on my way to Pinx, made a quick stop at the Mayfair to pick up an Entenmann's raspberry Danish twist—even though I'd already had half a muffin—several Budget Gourmets, peanut butter, bread and orange marmalade. After pulling into the parking lot behind the store, I left everything in the trunk except the Danish and walked into Pinx just as we were about to open.

Mikey was angry. I could tell from the look on his face. "She's late."

"Missy? She's not supposed to be here until noon."

"She was a half-hour late yesterday and then took an hour for lunch. I told her to come in early to make up for it. She's supposed to be here."

"You can't do that, Mikey. She's supposed to work from noon until eight thirty with a half-hour lunch and two fifteen-minute breaks. If she works an extra hour, then I have to pay her overtime."

"No you don't. It's the hour she owes you from yesterday."

"We have to pay people for the hours they work on the days that they work them. Anything else is illegal."

"It shouldn't be illegal."

"Well, it is. And you're not the one who'd get in trouble. I'd get in trouble. So stop it."

I set the Mayfair bag onto the counter and said, "I got Entenmann's."

"Raspberry Danish?"

"Yes."

Mikey reached under the counter for some napkins and a plastic knife, while I took the Danish out of the bag.

"What do I do when Missy shows up?"

"Don't yell at her for being late. And make sure she doesn't work more than eight hours. So either she takes a long lunch or she goes home early."

Mikey would have frowned, but he'd already cut a piece of the Danish and was taking a bite of it. I cut myself a small piece and put it on a napkin. Picking up my coffee, I started back to my office.

"There's a couple days of mail on your desk and a new shipment of videos."

"Did you open the videos?"

"Not really."

That meant yes. I rolled my eyes and walked back to my office. Sitting on my desk was the already opened box. After setting down my coffee and the Danish, I dug through the box and found the packing slip. As I pulled the videos out I checked them against the slip. There were three copies each of *Father of the Bride* and *For the Boys*, two copies of *Into the Night*, *The Hidden*, *House of Games* and *Electric Dreams*. And one copy of *Belly of an Architect*, which looked too artsy for it to rent very often.

Then I turned my attention to the mail. Most of it was junk. There were a couple of bills that I didn't even bother to open and a letter from my insurance agent. The last was a quote telling me what it would cost to insure myself and six of my employees. Three hundred and twenty-seven dollars and forty-eight cents. Each. That was a lot better than the one thousand ninety-two dollars I'd pay on my own. The problem was I had to convince all of my employees to take the insurance, and convince them that three hundred twenty-seven dollars would be easy for them to pay—even though it was close to one week's salary for each of us. I was pretty sure I wasn't going to be able to do that. I was also pretty sure I only had five employees. This was a mess.

How did sick people in this country survive?

I sat down and took my pills out of my pocket, opened up the tissue and placed them on my desk. I ate the Danish in a couple of bites. It actually tasted good. Then I washed my pills down with tepid coffee.

Before I finished swallowing, the phone was ringing. I decided not to answer since I was kind of occupied. A minute or so later, the intercom buzzed. I picked it up and Mickey told me it was my friend Marc. I thanked him and hung up. Then I clicked over to Marc.

"What's up?"

"I called SAG and got the name of Brick Masters' agent. I told my boss I had a doctor's appointment and she's giving me the afternoon off. Of course, she thinks I'm really skipping out to start Pride weekend early, but that's fine, too. Do you want me to come pick you up and we'll go talk to the agent?"

"Why not just call him on the phone?"

"It's easier for people to lie over the phone, don't you think?"

I had the feeling that might be true. I really shouldn't go, though. Not with Mikey and Missy at each other's throats. I thought about what my afternoon might be like and said, "Um, yeah, pick me up."

I hung up and wiped the crumbs off my desk. Taking a deep breath, I walked out to the front. Missy was there looking sullen and miserable behind the counter with Mikey.

I could only see one customer, though there might have been another in the Adult Section. That section took up most of one end of the store and could only be entered through a couple of louvered half-doors, giving it the feeling of entering a Wild West saloon.

Stopping in front of the counter, I looked at both of my employees. "I have to go out for the afternoon. Here's the thing: You two need to learn to get along. What that means exactly is, Mikey you're going to stop trying to manage Missy. You're not in charge here, I am. And Missy, you're going to listen to Mikey when he has a good idea. He's a smart guy and will probably save you from making mistakes you don't want to make. Are we clear?"

They both looked at me like I was an alien in a Steven Spielberg movie. Then began nodding vigorously.

"You can take the videos off my desk and input them into the system. Try to get them on the shelves by four if you can. It would be nice if they'd rent tonight."

That got me more nodding. I said good-bye and walked out of the store. I went over to Taco Maria and ordered a chicken enchilada. I needed something in my stomach besides Entenmann's. I also needed to take a few deep breaths. I probably hadn't said anything even remotely forceful to my staff since Jeffer died. And now I felt like kind of an asshole. I was running off for the rest of the afternoon, and maybe even the day since I was supposed to go to New York, New York later. Somehow Mikey and Missy were going to have to get along until Carl and Denny got there at six o'clock. Maybe the thing with Brick's agent wouldn't take too long and I could pop back in.

About forty minutes later I was standing out in front of Taco Mario's, burping up enchilada/root beer-flavored gas as Marc pulled up in his silver Infiniti. I climbed in and appreciated the leather seats, which were not only nicer than the cloth seats in my car but also moved in directions my Nissan could not even imagine.

"His agent's over in Burbank," Marc said. "1302 North Victory Boulevard. There's a Thomas Guide in the glove compartment. Can you look it up?"

"Sure."

I opened the glove compartment and took out the inch-and-a-half thick Thomas Guide. I flipped through the pages until I found Burbank and then started looking for Victory. At first it wasn't there; then it was everywhere. There was a South Victory, North Victory, West Victory and Victory Place.

"Did you say north?" I asked.

"I did."

"Okay, I got it."

"I'm going to take the 5, where do I get off?"

"Burbank Boulevard."

"And then?"

"We're going to go south."

"Okay."

We were only a few blocks from the highway. We just had to stay on Hyperion until it went under the freeway. As soon as it did, there was an entrance that would get us going in the right direction.

"So SAG just gives out people's agents?" I asked.

"Sure. I mean, I might have said I was a casting director. Actors usually want you to be able to reach them in some way."

"What do you think his agent might know?"

"It depends on the agent. Some of them want to be very close to you and know everything about you. Like they want to be your parents. Others really don't want to know much about you at all. You're just a commodity to them."

"Why do you know so much about agents?"

"I had one from seventy-four to seventy-eight."

"Why did you have an agent?"

"*I* was a teenage actor." The way he said it made it sound like the title of an expose or a bad sci-fi movie from the fifties.

"Were you in anything?"

"Of course I was. I wouldn't have had an agent for nearly five years if I wasn't."

"Oh, sorry. It's just, well, I know a lot of movies—"

"I was in three movies. Yes, you have them at your store and no, I'm not telling you what they are. My big claim to fame though was a kids' show called *Kapowie*."

"I don't remember that."

"Of course you don't remember it. We're almost the same age. I was thirteen, fourteen when it was on. It was aimed at pre-teens. Mostly we sang and danced about how important it was to be nice to each other. And sometimes we'd teach kids how to do crafts or cook or fix their own bikes. It was a really weird show."

I was looking at Marc in a whole new light. He wasn't just my nice neighbor who was a little thick in the middle and rushing toward an early middle age. Now he was Marc, a former child-actor. It really shouldn't have made him more interesting, but it sort of did.

"So which kind was your agent?"

"I had three. The first one wanted to be my mother. She was with a very small agency, specialized in kids and mothered us all. The second one was going to make me a big star and was with a really good agency. He barely spoke to me after signing me. And then the third one was the worst. She'd been an actress herself and I think she secretly hated when her clients got work so she sort of made sure we didn't."

"Do you ever want to go back to it?"

"God no. And even if I did, Louis would kill me."

"Why would he kill you?"

"You can't figure that out? Louis is the star in our relationship. He's the one who's always reaching out and meeting people, inviting them to dinner, making dinner. He's got the funnier jokes and the more interesting stories. I'm just in the background, which is really where I'd rather be."

I didn't think that was as true as he thought it was. But I could see how being a working actor might upset anyone's relationship. It was about then that I realized I couldn't remember being with Marc without Louis. It was a funny, awkward kind of feeling.

Griffith Park was on our left and the industrial backside of Glendale on our right. We crossed the 134 and Burbank Boulevard started showing up on the signs. Western Ave 3. Alameda Ave 2. Burbank Blvd 1.

We zipped along and then IKEA was on our right. The very first one in California. Marc said, "Louis is obsessed with IKEA."

I was well aware of Louis' love for IKEA. He loved the white candles that came twenty-five in a box for a tiny price. He loved the tea towels in packs of five, the inexpensive frames in strange and un-useful sizes, and the down comforters that came with brightly patterned duvet covers. I couldn't exactly criticize since I owned a POONG chair.

"Personally," Marc said, "I don't think it's much more than a Swedish Pic N' Save."

I smiled. He'd used that joke before.

And then we were pulling off the freeway, which forced me to keep a closer eye on the Thomas Guide.

"It's up on the right," I said. "The second right."

"I see it," Marc said, working his way over to the lane furthest to the right.

Just a few minutes later we were pulling into a failed two-story office complex from the late fifties. The building had a Jetson-style brass railing on the second floor and an awning style roof that hung out over the walkway. The parking lot was large, much too ambitious for the building, its only other tenant a carpenter's local union office.

Getting out of the car, it was noticeably hotter than when we'd gotten in. Just simply driving into the valley meant a temperature increase of ten degrees.

"He's in 203," Marc said, leading me up the stairs. "Arthur Feldman and Associates. I doubt there are any associates."

His office was second from last and didn't have his name on the door. Marc knocked and a moment later we heard a voice say, "Come in." We did.

Inside was a single office. On one side was a large mahogany desk piled with scripts. On the other, near the door, was a card table, where I assumed Mr. Feldman would put a secretary when times were good. It didn't look like times had been good in a long while.

Behind the desk was Arthur Feldman, an elderly man without a single hair on his head and an impressive collection of liver spots. He was well over eighty.

"Mr. Feldman?" Marc said.

"Arthur, please." He quickly looked Marc up and down and then said, "No. They're not looking for you. Not right now. You're not ready for character work; you're too young. Come back in five years." Then looking at me, he said, "This one, maybe."

He was making me feel uncomfortable. "We're not actors, Mr. Feldman," I said. "My name is Noah Valentine."

"Good name. Are you sure—?"

"And I'm Marc Rucker."

"No, that we'll have to change."

"We'd like to ask a few questions about Brick Masters," Marc said.

"Are you friends of his?" Arthur asked. "Were you in a show with him? He did that show at, what's that little theater called—?"

"We're not actors," I said, again. "Brick's body was left in the courtyard of our building. We're kind of curious about who might have killed him."

"Yes, well, I'd like to know that too."

"We're just wondering if you could tell us about Brick."

"Like, was that really his name?" Marc added.

"Well, yes, it was his name. His mother was a big fan of all those Rocks and Tabs and Troys back in the day. And she always wanted him to be an actor."

"What else did you know about him?" I asked.

"He wasn't a very good actor, I know that."

"Why did you represent him if he wasn't a good actor?"

"He was a face. His pictures got him places. If he could have learned to talk he would have gone places."

"Do you know Anthony Mercer?" Marc asked.

"The police were here, they asked about him too. I've heard of Mercy Costumes, of course. I've had to send my actors there for fittings. But no, I don't know him."

"Did Brick?"

Arthur shrugged.

"Was Brick gay?" Marc asked and then had to clear his throat.

"Oh, I don't know about that. Some of these boys they're what they need to be, you know?"

"Was he what he needed to be?" I asked.

Again the shrug. The phone rang and Arthur said, "Excuse

me a moment, I have to get this. My secretary is out with a bad cold."

Marc and I looked at each other. I raised my eyebrows, he raised his in return. Arthur was on the phone getting bad news about a client. "Oh, no, no, she never reads well the first time. You have to give her a callback. She's better if you give her a callback."

With nothing better to do, I looked around the office.

"You won't be sorry, trust me. Uh-huh, uh-huh."

On the walls of his office were posters from films that he directed in the forties and fifties. They had titles like *Midnight Lady*, *Boys of Tuskegee* and *A Death in Harlem*. They boasted "all-colored" casts and at the bottom of each poster it said, "directed by Arthur Feldman."

"I bet you've never heard of any of those pictures, have you?" he said as he hung up the phone.

"No sir, I haven't." And since I owned a video store that was saying something.

"They're race movies. We used to make them to show to the negroes in the South. They couldn't go to the white theaters, so they had their own theaters and for a while they had their own movies to show in them."

"And you directed those?"

"Many of them, yes. And it wasn't just colored films, I did a couple of Chinaman films in the thirties, but I didn't like those as much." He smiled, remembering something. "See, my third wife was a Negress. Starred in a couple of the movies I made. Amazing woman. If you have the chance to marry a Negress, take it. You won't be sorry."

Marc and I smiled politely. There was something about his tone that made me feel like he spent most of his time somewhere where the civil rights movement hadn't happened yet.

"And you're an agent now," I said, trying to pull him back to the present.

"Oh, I've done everything. People think I didn't amount to much since I never got famous, but that's not true. Lots of people in Hollywood don't get famous, but we still make a good living, have a good life." I wondered how true that was since it seemed clear he should have retired decades ago.

"What about Hollywood Costume?" Marc asked. "Did Brick have anything to do with them?"

Arthur got up from the chair, something that was a bit challenging for him. He might have been a tall man once, but now he couldn't stand fully erect. A few feet from his desk was a filing cabinet. He pulled out a drawer and looked for a file.

When he found the one he wanted, he opened it.

"Here it is. Brick did two weeks on *The Edge of Light*. Terrible. You never saw anyone so scared. He played a robber holding half the cast hostage in a diner. He was more afraid than they were. Do you watch the show?"

"We both work in the daytime," Marc said. Of course, we were there in the daytime, so he added, "Normally."

"Why is it important that he worked on a soap?" I asked.

"The costume designer was the guy from Hollywood Costume. Bob Martin."

"Billy Martinez?"

"Yeah, that's it."

13

MARC AND I WALKED INTO NEW YORK, NEW YORK at about six o'clock. It was already packed. The decorations they'd put up for Pride the week before were beginning to look a little wilted. I could see a half dozen popped balloons and another half dozen that had simply withered. Cher was playing on the jukebox saving up her tears, and then before we'd had a chance to get our drinks a band I didn't know wanted to talk about sex.

We'd had plenty of time to stop at home and change. Marc wore a thick Polo shirt with a single stripe across the chest which somehow seemed to tame his expanding belly, jeans and a pair of Vans. I wore a black mock turtleneck, Levis and my Docs. I had a jean jacket in the car for when it got cold. And it would get cold; it was probably eighty, but as soon as the sun went down it would drop twenty degrees.

Marc got a Kettle One and soda, and offered me his two-for-one. I should have had just a soda, but it was easier to just say yes. Drinks in hand, we looked around for a spot to stand, or at least a spot we could elbow our way into.

"Do you think Tall, Dark and Delicious knows about the connection between Brick and Hollywood Costume?" Marc yelled over the crowd and the music.

"I don't know. He didn't mention it. Actually, he didn't

mention very much at all. He doesn't want to talk to me about the case."

"But he does want to talk to you?"

I was saved from his leading question by Leon's arrival. He wore a gray suit and a thin layer of sweat. "I saw Louis in the parking lot. In fact, I think I stole his space. He may have to park out on Fletcher."

Before Leon could leave to get a drink at the bar, Tina walked up.

"Sorry I'm late. I was at the agency today. Friday meetings." Tina got to work at home most of the time, one of the few things she liked about her job. She wore a gray suit with a pressed white shirt and a black ribbon in place of a tie. You might have thought she was a banker except that instead of slacks or a skirt, the suit boasted a pair of knee length shorts with a nice cuff at the hem.

I couldn't help myself, I was staring at the shorts. Tina caught me and said, "Don't gawk. It was on sale, all right?"

"It's um, fashionable," I said.

Too fashionable. The kind of fashionable that designers won praise for sending down a runway but women, for the most part, resisted.

"I'm getting a drink, what do you want?" Leon asked.

"Compari and soda?"

"How about a Kettle One and cranberry? On the house."

"Um, sure."

And then Leon was swallowed up by the crowd.

"Ugh, I have to read that new biography about Princess Di," Tina said. "Some producer thinks it would be a great vehicle for Meg Ryan. Meg Ryan! And so *I* have to read it. I mean, my job is ridiculous. I don't have to read a word to tell them it's a terrible idea. The book is supposed to be very gossipy, though, so it might not be too bad a read—if I can just get Meg Ryan out of my head."

"What is it you do?" Marc asked.

"Oh, sorry, I'm a reader for A&W—Artists & Writers, not the root beer. Do you know what a reader does?"

"I think so," Marc said. It did seem fairly obvious.

Louis came in. He'd stopped at home and was wearing a brightly patterned silk shirt and khaki shorts. He saw that we all had drinks and asked Marc, "What are you drinking?"

"Kettle One and soda."

He nodded, then turned and went up to the bar.

"I can't believe this place is so crowded all the time," Tina said. "I thought all the gay boys lived in West Hollywood."

"Oh, God no," said Marc. "Southern California has a particular gay migratory pattern. When you're young you live in West Hollywood, when you tire of the glitz and the glamour you move to Silver Lake, when you're ready to settle down it's Long Beach, and when it's time to retire you're off to Palm Springs."

"Is that true?" she asked me.

"Here you go," Leon said as he handed Tina her free drink. "I talked to Ford Wheeler!"

"Who is he again?" I asked.

"Oh my Lordy!" Leon crowed in imitation.

"Ah." To Tina, I said, "Costume designer for *The Service*. Says 'Oh my Lordy' a lot."

"Anyway, he says that Billy Martinez might very well be the one who set Brick and Anthony up on a date."

"We just established that Billy and Brick may have known each other. Brick was on *The Edge of Light* for two weeks. Billy does the costumes," Marc said.

"Well there you go," Leon said.

"But does it make sense?" I asked. "Weren't Billy and Anthony enemies?"

Louis was back with two drinks. He used his free drink to top off Marc's and my drinks. "What did I miss?"

"Leon learned that Billy Martinez set up the date between Brick and Anthony," Marc said. "We learned that Billy Martinez and Brick probably knew each other."

"I'm not sure any of this makes sense," I said, sticking to my guns.

"But he was trying to buy Mercy Costumes, so maybe

Anthony thought Billy was trying to make nice?" Leon suggested.

"I don't think I'd sell my business to someone just because they got me a date no matter how pretty the date was," Tina said.

"Maybe the date was just to distract Anthony," Louis guessed.

"For what reason?" Marc asked.

"Well, the people who worked for Anthony said they had to clean up a mess. So, maybe it *was* about the dress. Anthony may have wanted to sell the dress in order to save his business. If Billy knew that Wilma was going to buy the dress, then maybe he was trying to steal it so that Anthony couldn't sell it, forcing him to sell Mercy Costumes to Martinez."

I had to admit that was an interesting theory, but I wasn't ready to settle on it. "What did you find out, Louis?"

"I struck out. People loved the lemon bars, but I wasn't able to get anyone to run Anthony's credit report. They did tell me we could go to the county clerk and find out if there are liens on the property."

"Anthony must have needed money. Detective O'Shea said he told people he was selling the dress. Why else would he want to sell a dress he'd had for years?" I didn't mention how little O'Shea wanted to share information with me.

"What about you, Tina?" Leon asked. "What did you find out?"

"Very little. I stopped in to see Robert when I got home last night, but he was on his way out and just wouldn't talk to me. And then this morning he wasn't there. He may not have come home. I'm not sure. I called him around lunchtime and we chatted for a minute or two. I tried to ask him how his job was going and if he was getting along with Billy, you know, to open up the subject, but suddenly he had to go. Some zipper emergency."

"Sounds like he has a boyfriend," Louis suggested.

"Yes, except he always tells me," Tina replied.

"He tells everyone," I agreed. Though he hadn't told me in ages.

"I have to say something," Tina announced. "If Billy was trying to steal the dress and force the sale, Robert couldn't have known anything about it. He's just not that sort of person. I mean, he might be discreet about something if his boss asked him, but not about burglary."

"A burglary that turned into a double murder," Marc corrected.

"That's the other thing about your theory, Louis," I said. "What went wrong? Why did Anthony end up dead?"

"And Brick a week later?" Marc added.

"Brick is easy," I said. "He knew whatever went wrong and got himself killed for it."

"And Anthony?"

None of us had an answer for that.

I did not have another drink. Well, not a whole one. We stayed at the bar for another two hours. The conversation turned to the election, which I was not paying much attention to. Tina was adamant that not only should Bush not get re-elected, but he should also go to prison for his part in the Iran-Contra cover-up. The rest of us thought that whole thing was over, but apparently there was an article about it in the morning paper and it was all still being investigated. Who knew?

Leon liked Bill Clinton but was sure no one in America would vote for a man who cheated on his wife and kept saying, "Look at Gary Hart!" The world all found out Clinton was a philanderer at the very start of the primaries, however, and now he was the candidate, so maybe it didn't matter.

"I think Bush will win," declared Louis. "Mainly because he's boring. America loves boring." And that started a whole other debate. When they finally stopped talking about politics, Louis suggested we all go to La Casita Grande and have dinner.

And margaritas. I begged off, planning to stop at Pinx on my way home.

I was right to put a jacket in the car. By the time I left the bar around eight thirty it was dark and less than seventy degrees. It was roughly a mile from the bar to the video store, so I was there in five minutes.

The after-work rush was just ending when I walked in. Carl and Denny were each checking out customers. Behind them, the TV was playing Channel 9 News. I went behind the counter to see what kind of mess Missy and Mikey left. It didn't look terrible. There was a stack of returned videos that needed to be input, but that could—I heard Carl say to his customer, "Would you like any lube with your rental?"

I looked up. The customer was a gentleman in his late forties who was renting one of our straight porn titles, *American Built*. My cheeks flushed. *Oh God, I was going to have to deal with this*. I was about to apologize when the man asked, "Well, um, what sort of stuff do you have?"

And then Carl was explaining in extensive detail what we had and which ones were better. He used phrases like, "This one is my favorite" and "I think you'd really like…" which when you thought about it was kind of ridiculous. I mean, this was an old gay guy giving a middle-aged straight guy homespun masturbatory advice.

The guy bought a small bottle of Wet to go with his rental and left. Denny had been waiting on a girl in her early thirties who was blushing. I was ready to apologize to her, but then she said to Denny, "Do you think I could get one of those too?"

I nearly threw my hands up into the air.

"Of course you can, darling," he said, reaching under the counter to retrieve a small bottle, throwing it into the plastic video bag.

I wasn't sure what to say. Honestly, I wasn't thrilled that Mikey's idea about upselling was working out. It made me very uncomfortable. But I had to be honest, it did seem to work.

"I'm glad you're here, darling," Denny said. "I was reading in the newspaper there are four more Marilyn Monroe videos coming out. You *have* to get them. The ones we have rent all the time."

"I think I might have already ordered them," I said. I'd explained to him before that what he saw in the newspaper about videos was actually old news and meant for consumers, but he didn't listen.

It wasn't a tough decision buying older films. They cost a third of what new releases cost, so they didn't have to rent as often to make their money back. Our other Marilyn tapes had been very profitable. Silent films didn't work, nor did classic foreign films, so I did avoid those.

I decided to ignore the question of selling lube and asked, "How were Mikey and Missy when you came in, had they killed each other?"

"Oh, they're so cute together," Carl said.

"Like brother and sister," Denny added.

As an only child, that idea would not have occurred to me. "All right then, so everything's under control."

"Oh yes, it's a smooth sailing ship," Carl replied.

"Why are you watching the news? Why don't you have a video in there?"

"Denny is terrified the riots will break out again," Carl said in a stage whisper.

"Me?! You're the one who bought enough canned goods to last through an apocalypse."

"And which one of us sent away for the Smith & Wesson catalog?"

"That wasn't because of the riots, that was because you get on my nerves."

That cracked them up. Killing each other was their idea of a joke. I came out from behind the counter and started looking around for a video to play. There were a couple of customers wandering around. Friday brought out the dateless singles. It was a big night for romantic comedies and porn.

Which gave me an idea. I looked through the classics section and found *Pillow Talk*. Mikey had probably not chosen it for the Hidden Treasures shelf because it was one of the classics that rented well. My plan was that it might draw the romantic comedy renters away from the newer films and toward the older ones. It was at least worth a try.

I was heading back to the counter when I heard Carl say, "Oh, thank God. They caught someone."

Both Carl and Denny were glued to the TV.

"What's going on?" I asked.

"They caught the person who murdered that costumer."

"Really? Who was it?" As I focused on the television the report ended and the anchorman moved on to a story about the governor predicting a budget disaster if the legislature didn't lower taxes immediately. Which was a little confusing. How could they lower taxes when they were already spending more than they had?

"Kelly something," Carl said.

"No that's not it," Denny said. "It was Gary something."

"Kerry? Was it Kerry?" I asked.

"Yes, that sounds right," Carl admitted. "Mesnick. Or Metzer. Or Meyer."

"He worked for Anthony?"

"Yes, that's what they said."

But Kerry couldn't possibly have done it, I thought. Something had gone very, very wrong.

14

Saturday morning, I was up really early and decided to listen to *Gypsy* while I cleaned my apartment. Jeffer had bought me the Tyne Daly version. We'd seen her do it at the Dorothy Chandler and I'd loved it. Had we gone on my birthday? I tried to remember. Jeffer was good at things like that. Birthday presents. Gestures.

Of course, I was also thinking about poor Kerry. He couldn't have killed Anthony. I wanted to call Detective O'Shea and ask why he arrested the kid, but he'd just think I was calling because I liked him and I really needed to send the message that I didn't like him. And that meant I couldn't call him.

Even though I was up early, Marc and Lewis were up earlier. I knocked on their door to see if they were around, but there was no answer. They'd probably gone out for breakfast before they spent the day looking at houses they couldn't quite afford.

Since there wasn't anyone to ask questions, or even anyone to talk to, I spent the morning dusting and straightening up as I listened to "You Gotta Have a Gimmick." The bedroom was easy since there wasn't much in there besides the bed. The duffle I used for laundry was full, so I needed to go to the laundromat. I'd go later on or Sunday maybe. No, Sunday was Pride. Monday, maybe. Anyway, I'd go soon. I had no choice.

The living room required a bit more straightening up. The love seat was wrapped in a black-and-purple cloth, which meant that it came unwrapped. I rewrapped it the way I wanted it. Then I folded the afghan my mother made and laid it over the back of the love seat. Now it looked inviting enough that I'd sit on it and mess it all up again.

The kitchen was basically clean because I used it so seldom. Well, there might have been some dust on the countertops but other than that it was spotless.

Should I maybe cook something sometime? Just to prove to myself I could still do it. It seemed like a good idea, except that I had enough trouble eating the leftovers Louis pushed on me without making my own. Of course, I could make something bland. Why had it been so easy to cook for Jeffer all those years and so hard to cook for myself? I tried to decide if I should even try to answer that question. Chances were I wouldn't like the answer.

My phone rang. My mother, right on time.

"I told Carolyn you met Wilma Wanderly and she did not believe me."

"Why would you lie about that?"

"That's what I said! Then she said she didn't think it was me who was lying. She said it was you."

"Why would I lie about it? I mean if I was going to lie about meeting movie stars why not someone popular, like Julia Roberts or Sharon Stone?"

"Oh, I hadn't thought of that. You're so smart."

I was glad my mother was making a friend, but I was beginning to wonder what kind of friend Carolyn really was.

"Now, I have to ask a question. Why a parade?"

"What?"

"It's your gay day soon, isn't it? Why do you have a parade?"

"Mom, it's not exactly a parade. I mean, it is, but it's also a demonstration."

"Like they did in the sixties? Oh my, that's worse."

"Actually it started as a riot."

"Oh I don't think people should riot. Or demonstrate."

"I guess we know whose side you'd have been on during the Revolutionary War."

"Of course we do. I'd have been on America's side."

"Well, no you wouldn't be. They were the ones rioting and demonstrating."

"That's not true."

"What do you think the Boston Tea Party was?"

She was quiet for a moment. She usually was when I made a point she didn't like.

"We've gotten off track," she said. "I was talking to Carolyn about gay day and she had questions I couldn't answer."

"Gay Pride, Mom. And why are you talking about it with Carolyn?"

"Well, it's next weekend."

No, it's tomorrow, I thought. But then something occurred to me. "You mean, it's next weekend in Grand Rapids."

"Yes, that's what I mean."

"You have Gay Pride in Grand Rapids?"

"Of course, this is the fourth year."

"Okay." This was news to me.

"Now, Carolyn wants to know why gays get a parade and other people don't."

"Other people get parades. Who's being parade deprived?"

"Well, Carolyn pointed out there's no parade for straight people."

"Mom, every other parade *is* for straight people. The gay parade is the only one that's not."

"Oh. I hadn't thought about it that way. I should write that down and tell Carolyn." She was quiet for a moment and I wondered if she'd actually gone off to write it down. "The other thing she says is that gays shouldn't be so in your face, you know, about sex and stuff."

"Really, that's what she says?"

"I don't think she means anything by it."

"Do you agree with her?"

"It's just, the pictures they show."

"What pictures?"

"You know, on the news. Half-naked men and such."

"Didn't you say Carolyn was always in your face about her grandchildren?"

"Yes, but—"

"And there are four of them?"

"Three and a half."

"You do remember how you get children, don't you?"

"Yes, but—"

"There are no buts, Mom. Straight people talk about sex all the time. They just don't call it talking about sex. They call it wholesome, but it's still about sex. Any time you ask if someone has a girlfriend—"

She was quiet for a long moment. I didn't know if I was convincing her. Then she said, "Let's talk about something else. *Housesitter* was not as good as I'd hoped it would be."

I took a deep breath and got off my soapbox.

"I'm sorry. I know you were looking forward to it."

"Carolyn loved it, but I don't know…I loved the house better than the movie. You should see it just for the house."

"I will see it. When it comes out on video."

"Oh, of course, you see everything."

"So, how's garden club?" I asked. This was my go-to question. Whenever I wanted my mother to talk and not ask me questions, I asked about her garden club. Typically, there was enough drama there to fuel a nighttime soap. But not today.

"Oh, I haven't been in weeks," she said.

"Why not?"

"I don't know. I've been busy with Carolyn and going to church with her. Everyone's so nice there. They have a potluck on Thursday nights and Bible study on Wednesday. There's a Friday night service for people who can't make it on Sunday. That's progressive, isn't it? I mean, it's supposedly a very conservative congregation, but I don't see what's so terrible about believing in old-fashioned—"

And then I stopped listening for at least five minutes. I wondered if I should call over to Mercy Costumes and see if Willow was there. She might know why Kerry was arrested.

Could Kerry have done it? He'd seemed gentle and a bit clueless when he came to the memorial. Not to mention, I was sure Anthony's date with Brick was set up by the killer. I doubted Kerry had set up the date. So that meant the date had nothing to do with Anthony's death. And what about the dress? Was it somewhere in the shop and Willow just hadn't found it yet? Did that, too, have nothing to do with Anthony's murder?

"Mom, I need to go to work soon," I said to my mother. It was a lie. On Saturdays I didn't go in until one or two. Mikey was alone during the day on Saturday, so I needed to go in so he could have lunch.

"All right, dear. One more thing, though. I'm thinking of coming out to visit for the holidays. What do you think? Or do you want to come here?"

"I don't know. Let me think about it," I said, frantic to find a way out of the conversation. I couldn't have her come to L.A. I took pills three times a day. I couldn't tell her they were vitamins, she wouldn't believe me. And I was sure she'd snoop through the medicine cabinet, which meant I'd have to hide my pills somewhere before she even got here.

I could go to Grand Rapids, I suppose, but I'd still have to find a way to hide my pills. And that's not even considering my appetite. She's bound to notice I don't eat a whole lot of food—and bound to say something about it every day, at every meal.

"All right, well, don't think about it too long. I know it's months and months away, but we should start looking at airfares soon."

"Okay. I'll think fast." Mainly about possible excuses for putting it off indefinitely.

After we hung up, I thought about getting ready for work. It was still early, though, and I hadn't finished my cleaning. I dusted the armoire that held my TV/VCR combo and CD player. Well, I played at dusting it. It was a little after ten. I wanted to be at Pinx by noon, that gave me enough time for a quick stop.

After a super quick shower, I towel dried my hair. When I was done I glanced in the bathroom mirror. My hair looked like a stack of twigs that someone forgot to set on fire. I didn't want to spend fifteen minutes trying to blow dry it and I wasn't in the mood to wear a hat, so I decided if anyone asked I'd tell them a head of hair that looked like kindling was the latest style.

I threw on a basic outfit of jeans, a work shirt and a silver skinny tie that used to be Jeffer's. I'd liked it enough that I'd stolen it from his closet. Then I was out the door and over to Sunset and Mariposa. I parked in the same spot Marc had parked in the week before. Taking a deep breath, I got out of the car and crossed over to the entrance of Mercy Costumes.

I struggled to organize my thoughts for a moment before I rang the bell. They didn't organize easily, so I gave up and just rang the bell. I had to wait long enough that I worried Willow wasn't there, but then she opened the door. She didn't say anything, just looked at me.

"Hi, how are you?" I said.

"Seriously?"

She walked away. I grabbed at the door so it didn't fall shut and lock. Once inside the cool, dark warehouse, I headed toward the center and the large worktable. The worktable was stacked with piles of costumes, each with a piece of notepaper on top. The little television wasn't tuned to a station, instead it showed the view from the camera outside. That was how she knew who was there before she answered the door.

Willow wore a couple of T-shirts under a ripped sweatshirt and gym shorts over a pair of tights.

I said, "Listen, Willow, I have a couple of quick questions."

"You're the one who passed out. Are you all right?"

"I'm fine. Thanks for asking. Can you tell me why the police arrested Kerry?"

Tears gathered in her eyes. "I don't know why they did that. Kerry wouldn't hurt anybody. He's not like that. He's really kind of sweet."

"The two of you were close?"

"Well, not like that. I mean, once after a party, but no, not..." I was really just wondering if they were friends. "It's a bummer he's not here," she continued. "We've still got four shows to do this week and it's just me."

"Uh-huh, that sounds awful," I said, cringing at my obvious insincerity. "When was Kerry arrested?"

"Yesterday morning. While they were searching the place."

"Why were they searching yesterday? Weren't they here before?"

She shrugged. "Yeah. They came back."

"And they found something? On their second visit?"

"I guess Kerry had the gun that killed Anthony. I heard him say he just took it home so he could try it out."

"Try it out? You mean fire it?"

"Yeah."

That meant there was probably gunpowder residue on some of his clothes. Not to mention his fingerprints all over the murder weapon.

"Is there a reason Kerry would kill Anthony?"

"No, not really."

"What's the not really part?"

"So that policewoman asked me a bunch of questions and she made a big deal about Anthony firing Kerry."

"It's not a big deal?" I guessed.

"No. Anthony fired Kerry three times a month. It didn't mean anything and it certainly didn't mean enough for Kerry to kill him."

"The night of the murder, Anthony sent you home early. Did you leave with Kerry?"

She shook her head.

I stood there for a minute not knowing what to say. I mean, from what Willow said it made sense that the police had arrested Kerry. He did look kind of guilty. But looking guilty wasn't the same thing as being guilty and my gut told me he didn't do it. Not that that meant anything. I'd been wrong about people before.

But it did still leave me with all the questions I'd had before. "This might seem like a weird question, but what kind of guys did Anthony like? Did he have a type?"

"Um, gosh…" she said, looking uncomfortable. I wasn't sure if that meant she didn't know or didn't know if she should tell me.

"Did the police ask anything like that?"

"Oh my God, no."

That was interesting. Why hadn't Detective O'Shea asked that? I mean, before he zeroed in on Kerry he should have asked that. I wondered if he might be afraid of seeming to know too much about gay guys. Not that he knew much at all. Leon was right, he was a gayby.

"So what do you know about Anthony's romantic life?"

"Well, he liked guys. He had a boyfriend when I started here, but they broke up."

"What was his boyfriend like?"

"He was kind of young. A black guy. He was nice—I mean, to me. I guess he wasn't very nice to Anthony."

The fact that his last boyfriend was black didn't mean that he wouldn't go out with a white guy, but it did mean he didn't *only* go out with white guys.

"How young is young?" I asked. "How much younger than Anthony?"

"A lot. Did you know Anthony was fifty? He didn't look that old to me."

I didn't know he was that old, but he could have been. If he and Dick Congdon had pulled *The Girl From Albany* dresses out of a dumpster in the seventies, well, he could easily be fifty.

"So his boyfriend was about your age?"

"Maybe. I mean, I never asked."

Willow was in her early twenties, so Anthony was seeing a guy who was around twenty-five years younger. Maybe that was his type. Young. Brick would fit into that category.

I was almost ready to thank her and say goodbye when something occurred to me: Why did Anthony need to be distracted? If that was the whole point of the date, why? Why did it have to happen that way? Why couldn't someone just break in during the middle of the night, steal the dress, and be done with it?

"What's the security like here?" I asked.

"Oh God, it's a pain. Anthony hired one of those security companies after the break-in."

"What break-in?"

"It was like a month ago, maybe a little longer."

"What did they take?"

"Nothing. They didn't really get in. There's an alarm and it was on. I mean, it worked, right? So why did he have to get the security company? It didn't make sense."

"Let me you ask you this, then…there's a camera outside the door, so you can actually see who's coming by on the TV, right?"

"Uh-huh."

"The night we stopped by you saw us standing out there, didn't you?"

"Uh-huh. You looked kind of silly staring up at the camera."

"Is there a videotape attached to that?"

"No, it's not that great."

"And if you're watching TV, then you can't see what's happening outside."

"If someone knocks we turn the channel."

"You can't see if someone was trying to break in?"

"No, but the door wasn't broken or anything."

"And there's an alarm? You mentioned that?"

"Uh-huh. We set it before we leave."

I thought about all that. If Brick was supposed to be the distraction, what was the plan? I walked back down the path between the costume racks to the door, opened it and took a good look. The door locked automatically but you could use a matchbook to keep it from locking, I guessed, and then some other person could come along, slip through the door, and hide out until everyone left.

But then something caught my eye, something that was even simpler. On the clothes rack right next to the door was a very large, brown men's sweater. I took the sleeve of the sweater and held it over the lock as I closed the door. It held the door open.

I walked back to the worktable. I looked at the small screen and saw that the door looked normal.

"What are you looking at?" Willow wanted to know.

"The door is open."

"No, it's not."

"I slipped the sleeve of a sweater into the doorjamb. It's open."

Willow squinted at the television. Then she shrugged, not seeing why it was important.

"That's how the killer got in. Brick slipped something into the doorjamb. Maybe even the same sweater I just used. Then he was supposed to distract Anthony while someone else came into the building. But something went wrong."

15

THE NEXT MORNING, I HAD A DREAM THAT WAS EXACTLY like a Roman Polanski dream sequence. It began with the rumbling of a volcano and natives about to throw a virgin into the bubbling crater. But then I was the virgin, so I was rather relieved when they dropped me and scurried away. Thunder boomed from a cloud above, and I was tossed into the air.

My eyes sprang open and I realized we were in the middle of an earthquake. I jumped out of bed and stood in the doorway between the bedroom and the living room. It was quite dark; I could barely see anything. A few moments later the quake was over. After the briefest pause, car alarms began to go off all over the neighborhood. And then, in the distance, sirens.

There was a relentless pounding somewhere nearby, making me wonder if someone was trapped beneath something heavy. But then I realized it was my own heart. I took a few fast, deep breaths. The clock radio on the shelf behind my bed read 4:58.

I walked out of the apartment and stood on the walkway outside my door. Below me in the courtyard, Louis and Marc were standing there in their pajamas. Marc had a lit cigarette in one hand.

"You okay?" Louis asked.

"I'm fine. You guys?"

"Bookcase fell over," Marc said. "Scared the crap out of me."

"I told you we should have bolted it to the wall," Louis said.

"No, you didn't. I told you and you ignored me."

"Well, the excitement's over," I said. "See you in a couple of hours."

Before I could go back inside, Louis yell-whispered, "Hey, they arrested someone for Anthony's murder."

"Yeah, I know. We'll talk about it later."

I went back in to go to sleep. It had taken me until almost two o'clock to fall asleep, which meant I had gotten a little less than three hours of real rest. If fell asleep quickly, I could get two more hours in before it was time to get up and get ready for Pride. The parade was an hour earlier this year, at eleven, so we were driving over to West Hollywood a little after nine to give us time to find a parking spot.

Climbing into bed, I pulled the covers up around my chin. It was in the sixties at night and I didn't like to turn the wall furnace on. I tried not to think about poor Kerry stuck in jail. I needed to talk to the boys about everything I'd found out, which was a lot. I started to make a mental list but then stopped. *Go to sleep.* I needed sleep. I needed it badly.

I let go of all my muscles, tried to relax, failed miserably, hugged the blanket close, and then the phone rang. I knew who it was. And I knew if I didn't answer she'd just call back in five minutes. I got out of bed and went into the living room. The phone was off its cradle, lying in the middle of the love seat. I picked it up, clicked on, and said, "Hi, Mom."

"It was on CNN. You've had an earthquake. 7.6. That's almost the big one. Are you all right?"

"Yes, I'm fine."

"Is the apartment still standing?"

"Didn't even break a dish." I left out the bookcase that fell over downstairs. It wouldn't help matters.

"Oh, thank God. Now, do you have food and water in case you can't get to the store?"

"I have food and water." Well, I had water. Coming out of

the tap. "But there's nothing to worry about. The power is on. I don't think the epicenter is very close to here."

"It was somewhere called Landers."

"See, I don't even know where that is, so it can't be very close. I have to go back to bed now."

"Back to bed, but it's eleven—oh dear, I've done it again. It's subtract three hours and I keep adding."

"It's okay. I'm going to say good night now."

"Sleep tight, sweetheart."

I got back into bed and closed my eyes. I was sure I wouldn't get back to sleep anytime soon, but it was good just to rest. And then my alarm went off and it was suddenly seven thirty.

Yes, I needed two hours to get ready to leave for Pride.

First, I made a cup of tea and a slice of toast for my breakfast. When it popped out of the toaster I spread peanut butter and marmalade on it. Protein and vitamin C. Sometime I should try making an egg for breakfast, which sounded simple enough, but not when I realized I'd have to buy a pan and a spatula and butter and a dozen eggs to do it. It was complicated; more complicated than I wanted to deal with just then.

I ate my breakfast, swallowed my pills, and then took a shower. After I dried off, I stood naked in front of my closet deciding what to wear. Eventually, I decided on a pair of black-and-white checked linen shorts and a white T-shirt with the poster art from *Gone With the Wind* on the front. I put on a pair of white socks with running shoes—it was going to be a long day with a lot of walking and I wanted my feet to be comfortable.

Then it was time to go back into the bathroom and do something with my hair. It was going to be hot outside. We weren't getting much in the way of June Gloom, so I knew by eleven it would be in the eighties. It wouldn't be too bad if I was inside, but we were going to be outside in the sun, sweating and wearing sunscreen. That meant my hair would be damp and sticking up straight by noon. I decided maybe I should just start out that way. I ran some gel through my hair and pushed it straight up as best I could.

And then the earth jumped. An aftershock, or maybe not an aftershock. It was pretty strong. It felt like an earthquake all of its own. I ran out of the bathroom, through the bedroom, into the living room. The apartment had begun to move, glassware in the kitchen began to clatter, the Hockney print on my wall slid sideways. I looked out at the L.A. basin. I could feel the floor moving beneath my feet and it felt like the whole building was a ship drifting along on a very uncertain sea.

And then it slowed, slowed some more and stopped. Just like earlier, car alarms were going off and sirens were starting in the distance. Down in the courtyard there was screaming. The woman who lived on the first floor in the back had rushed out, "IT'S THE END OF THE WORLD! IT'S THE END OF THE WORLD! GOD'S VENGEANCE HAS ARRIVED!"

The man she lived with, and whom I'm fairly certain she punched every now and then, said, "It's just an earthquake, Loretta."

"Oh, what do you know," she yelled at him and then went back inside.

Nothing was broken. The pictures hadn't even come off the walls. After I straightened the Hockney, I turned on the television and found out that the second quake was not an aftershock but actually was its own quake. Which was exactly how it felt. The earlier quake was 7.4 and located about a hundred miles from L.A. This one was around 7 and they hadn't yet announced the epicenter.

The phone rang again. "Hi, Mom," I said. "I'm fine."

"Don't make fun of me. Your son hasn't had *two* earthquakes in one day."

"I'm not making fun of you." I wanted to, but I wasn't.

"Was this as bad as the first one? I was watching CNN and this woman was talking about the first earthquake and then this one started. She looked terrified."

"Well, she would be," I said. "She's sitting under a half a ton of lighting equipment."

"Carolyn called me. She doesn't know how you can live in California. The earthquakes, the riots, the fires, the mudslides. And the people; Carolyn despises hippies."

"Hippies? Mom, it's not the sixties. Is your friend related to Archie Bunker?"

"Don't be silly. Archie Bunker is a fictional character. They can't be related."

"There are no hippies, Mom. They got bored and invented computers."

"Really? Are you sure?"

"Okay, well, I have to go now."

"All right then. You be careful."

It was early, but I was a little bored so I went downstairs. Standing outside Marc and Louis' open door, I said, "Knock, knock."

"Come in," Louis called out.

I walked in and glanced around. In the living room, there were four comfortable chairs in a conversational grouping around a coffee table and a small bookcase in the same place that I had one, looking just like it did the last time I'd seen it. The place looked neat and clean, you'd have no idea it had been through two earthquakes in the last few hours.

"I thought you said the bookcase fell over."

"It did. We picked it up," Louis said. "Sit down. Do you want a piece of coffeecake? A cup of tea?"

"I'll have a cup of tea," I said, sitting down at the café table in the dining area off the kitchen. Marc was munching on a piece of coffeecake.

As he filled the kettle and put it on the stove, Louis said, "So, have you talked to Tall, Dark and Delicious about why he arrested Kerry?"

"No. I did talk to Willow, though."

"It was in the newspaper," Marc said. "They found the murder weapon with Kerry's fingerprints."

"And he'd just been fired," Louis added.

"I don't think he did it, though. Willow said he just took the gun home to try it out."

"That's so L.A.," Marc said. Many of our neighbors had a habit of shooting off guns in their backyards and it wasn't all that uncommon for stray bullets to find a victim.

"You don't think he did it?" Louis asked.

"No. I don't. I might believe it if it weren't for Brick Masters being there—"

"And ending up dead," Marc added.

"Yeah," Louis agreed. "And there's no reason for Kerry to leave Brick's body in our courtyard."

"You're going to need to talk to Detective Tall, Dark and Delicious."

"Why can't someone else do that?"

"You're the one he listens to. You're the one he likes."

"He thinks the main reason I've gotten involved is because I have a crush on him."

"And that's a problem because?" Louis asked.

"That's a problem because it's a problem," I said, trying to be forceful. And it must have worked because Marc and Louis gave each other a look and went back to their coffee cake.

After chewing for a moment, Marc said, "Okay."

Leon was waiting in front of his apartment building wearing dark, dark sunglasses. He was also wearing madras shorts, a white short-sleeved shirt and sandals. In one hand, he held a big straw hat, the kind elderly women wore for gardening. He climbed into the car saying, "Tell me again, why am I awake at this ungodly hour?"

"The parade starts at eleven. We need to leave Silver Lake by nine thirty to have any hope of parking and finding a good place to stand."

"I think they're insane. I've never been proud of anything this early on a Sunday morning."

Marc reached into the cooler they'd brought and got out a sippy cup shaped like a puppy. He extended a hand toward the back seat and Leon took the cup.

"Is there alcohol in this?" Leon asked. It looked like orange juice, though it was probably orange juice and something else.

"Yes."

"Nectar of the gods."

"Do you want one, Noah?"

"Do you have one without alcohol?"

"Sorry they're premixed. Do you want a bottle of water?"

"Yes, thanks."

Then Marc got out the sunscreen and we all slathered some on (Louis at a red light) even though I, at least, had put some on at home.

"I work with these two black gals, they're hysterical—well, actually they think I'm hysterical and I gravitate to people who think I'm funny—anyway, we go and get coffee and a muffin every day at ten- fifteen, and every time we walk by another black person they say 'hi' and afterwards I ask if they know each other and they don't. Apparently, black people say 'hello' to each other."

"Why do you think that's weird?" Louis asked.

"Gay people don't say hello to each other. We barely speak to each other."

"We don't always know, though."

"Exactly. And that's my favorite thing about Pride. Tomorrow is the day I go around saying hello to all the gay boys at work. All the pretty gay boys with their painful pink sunburns."

"You mean you say hello to all the white gay boys," Marc pointed out.

"True. But all the black and Hispanic ones say hello to me, since no matter how hard I try I'll be scorched by noon."

Traffic on Santa Monica Boulevard was already bad, so we went north a couple of blocks to Sunset and cut across the Hollywood flats.

"Do you have a parking strategy?" Marc asked Louis.

"I think we're going to end up above Sunset."

"Oh my God, I'm not sure I can walk that far," Leon said.

"What on Earth did you do last night?" Marc asked.

"I don't know. I only remember it was really, really fun."

"Where does the parade start?" I asked. We were now in the thick of Hollywood.

"Somewhere after Fairfax," Marc said.

Leon held up his sippy cup as though seeing it for the first time. "What a clever idea."

"Never underestimate the ingenuity of an alcoholic."

"Louis, you are not an alcoholic."

"The sippy cup was actually my ex's idea," Louis explained. "He was a robust social drinker."

There were occasionally hints about Louis' ex making me wonder if he sensed the trouble I'd had with Jeffer. Certainly, he'd always been, I don't know the right word, *kind* about Jeffer? He never asked too many questions and never let it matter that he didn't know very much about what happened. Of course, neither did Marc. It was something they seemed to silently agree on. Leon, on the other hand, did sometimes ask direct questions I did my best to deflect.

We started looking for a parking place in earnest. First we tried south of Sunset, checking block after block to no avail. Then we went north and found a spot on a street that was quickly climbing a hill.

"Everyone remember that the car is on King's Road."

They all refilled their sippy cups, since the cooler was staying in the car, and I got a new bottle of water. We got out of the car and Louis locked the doors. As soon as we crossed Sunset, we started to see other people on their way down to Santa Monica Boulevard for the parade. Fairfax was closed when we drove by, and we could see that's where the participants were gathering.

"What time is it?" I asked.

"A little after ten thirty," Marc said. It had taken an hour to pick up Leon and find a parking place. That might not have seemed like a lot, but we only lived a few miles away. The joys of city life.

"Did the earthquake wake you, Leon?" Louis asked.

"There was an earthquake this morning? How disappointing. I thought I'd finally found a man who could make the earth move."

Rolling his eyes at Leon's comment, Marc asked, "Are we staying together or are we going our own way?"

"Staying together," I said as Leon said, "Going our own way."

"Okay," Louis said. "Whatever we decide to do, how about we meet back at the car at two o'clock."

I didn't have a watch, but I could certainly stop someone and ask the time. "Sounds great."

When we got to Santa Monica Boulevard, I was shocked by the size of the crowd. I looked east down Santa Monica past the huge tile place and as far as I could see the street was lined with people. The sidewalks were full, while the curb was covered with those who'd already claimed spots.

"Let's go this way," Louis said and we turned west. That direction was even more crowded. The street in front of Barney's Beanery, which angled toward Santa Monica, was awash with people. On the sidewalk, we had to fight our way through.

"Oh my God," I said. "This is like happy hour at New York, New York except it goes on forever."

"Speaking of earthquakes," Leon said, even though we weren't. "Can you imagine how happy Jerry Falwell would be if the earth opened up and swallowed us all?"

"Oh God," said Louis. "The poor man would come in his pants."

"Imagine the money he'd make," Marc said. "He'd be able to sell tickets to heaven."

"How far down do we want to go?" Louis asked.

"Well, I think we should go as far as the bars, my sippy cup is only going to last so long," Leon said.

"Everyone is going to want to be in front of the bars," Marc said.

"Well, at least to the car wash then. I can slip down to Trunks when things get dull."

"Isn't that a hustler bar?" Louis asked.

"Not in at least a decade. And you're dating yourself. No

one calls them hustlers anymore. They're escorts, and you order them out of the back of *Frontiers*." Then Leon's face blanched behind his sunglasses. "Oh God, everyone look to the left. Mortal enemy on the right at three o'clock."

Each one of us looked to the right. There was a rather innocuous looking blond woman appearing kind of lost. She walked away from us. Leon took a peek and decided the coast was clear.

"That's one thing I hate about Pride. If you're looking for your dearest friend in the world you'll never find him. You will, however, find all of your ex-lovers and most of your former friends."

Ten minutes later, we were standing in front of the car wash. Leon had gone off to get a drink. It was hot; the sky was clear and brilliantly blue. Guys were taking off their shirts already. There were half a dozen people between us and Santa Monica Boulevard, people who'd staked out their claim hours ago, many with folding chairs.

The parade was starting. If I stood on my tippy-toes I could see a small red convertible about a block away. Louis' eyes must have been better than mine, because he said, "Look, there's Derwood."

It took me a minute to figure out what he was saying, but then I remembered my childhood afterschool viewing and said, "Darrin Stephens?"

"And Samantha," Marc said. "They're grand marshals."

The car rode by. The two actors smiled and waved, and looked much older than they used to. I swear she wiggled her nose.

"What is going on with her hair?" Louis asked.

Elizabeth Montgomery had her hair cut in a ball of curls, vastly differently from the sleek up-flip she'd worn twenty-five years before on her show. But she wasn't the reason they were grand marshals. Dick Sargent had recently come out and that had earned him the spot. Apparently, she was his plus one.

Behind them were several cars with dignitaries: the mayor of West Hollywood, a state assemblyman, the pastor from some church. Then Dykes on Bikes roared by, a marching band, a rifle corps spinning wooden rifles. The sun was getting hotter and hotter, and by noon it was well over ninety. I'd drunk my water and needed to get some more.

"We're going to go find the fundies and heckle them," Louis said. Each year there was a small, dedicated group of Christians who stood along the parade route with signs that announced we were all going to hell if we didn't immediately repent.

"Really?" I said. The idea of engaging them did not appeal to me.

"You're a little red in the face," Louis said. "Why don't you go down to Trunks and get a cool drink. Leon's probably down there. We'll look for you there."

And then they were gone. I went back to watching the parade. Signs that mentioned the morning's earthquakes were popular. An older woman carried a sign that said, "I quake with love for my lesbian daughter." The West Hollywood Cheerleaders made a cheer out of "Shake, Rattle and Roll."

I did need some water, and maybe make a trip to the men's room. I started walking toward Trunks and found myself looking at the most gorgeous man I'd seen in a long time. He wore a pair of work boots with white socks, cutoffs and a tank top stuffed in his back pocket. His skin was brown and glistening. I didn't even have to get near him to know he smelled of coconuts and lazy afternoons. I looked up into his caramel-colored eyes and said, "Crap."

"Hello, Noah."

"Detective O'Shea."

"I'm not on duty. You could try calling me Javier."

"That would be confusing." Then I glanced around at where we were: people waving rainbow flags, two men dressed as nuns roller-skating down the street. "Aren't you afraid someone will spot you?"

"A crowd like this is one of the most anonymous places in the world."

"Not that anonymous. You ran into me."

"Well, I was kind of looking for you."

"Seriously? You thought you'd find me today?"

"I'm a detective, remember?"

"How did you detect where I was?"

"You had to drive over here. Unless you left at six this morning, you weren't going to get good parking. That meant you wouldn't be very close to the festival end of things. You're kind of pale, so I figured you'd be on the shadier side of the street. So you see, right there I've already cut it down to ten or twelve blocks."

I suspected there was something to Leon's theory about running into people you didn't want to see, while being unable to find people you did.

"How long have you been looking for me?"

"About an hour," he admitted.

I was trying really hard not to look below his chin. I also needed to stop sweating. And remember to breathe.

Clearing my throat, I changed the subject. "Why did you arrest Kerry? You don't really think he killed Anthony."

"It isn't about what I 'think,' it's about what the evidence shows. And the evidence shows that Kerry killed his boss after he was fired."

"Is that what Kerry says?"

"You know I can't talk to you about the case."

"And you have no evidence that Kerry killed Brick."

"I can't talk to you about that case, either."

"You said it yourself, whoever killed Brick left his body in our courtyard to scare us. He had to think we were closing in on him. Kerry would never have thought that."

"But he was there at the brunch. He knew you were asking questions. He knew you might get around to asking about him."

I had a hard time putting that together with the somewhat dim-witted kid I'd met.

"The blue dress is missing, you know. Whoever killed Anthony has it. Did you find it at Kerry's place?"

He wasn't going to tell me but the answer was clearly no.

"Someone tried to break into Mercy Costumes maybe six

weeks ago, but the security there was too good, so they came up with a better plan. Whoever it was set Anthony up on the date with Brick so that Brick would distract him. Brick left a matchbook or something in the door to keep it from locking. That allowed someone to follow him in, someone who was going to wait until Anthony and Brick left and then search for the blue dress. But something went wrong."

O'Shea just stared at me. Finally he said, "That's an interesting theory. But you're guessing. And that's fine for you, you own a video store. I'm a policeman; I have to deal in facts."

"The break-in is a fact."

"Yes, I have a police report on that."

I went back over what I'd just said looking for more actual facts. "It's a fact that Anthony was set up on a date with Brick."

"Is it? Didn't that information come from Kerry?"

I couldn't really remember. Kerry had definitely been the one to provide Brick's name. Well, his first name. But I'm not sure if he mentioned that the date was a setup.

"I need to get some water. And maybe a soda. So I guess I'll see you around."

"Hey, don't run away. I want to ask you something."

"I'm kind of thirsty."

"Listen. They're showing this old movie, *Adam's Rib* in West L.A. You want to go?"

We had *Adam's Rib* on VHS, but still it raised an interesting question, "You like old movies?"

"I might. You like them, don't you?"

That was very considerate, I guess. And it was just a movie. Nothing would happen. We'd sit in the dark together. And that would be it.

"It's not a good idea."

I knew he was going to ask me why it wasn't a good idea, and I was too busy trying to think up a good excuse to realize he'd taken a couple of steps closer to me and what that might mean.

Slipping an arm around me he lifted me an inch off the ground and kissed me. His lips were firm but very smooth. He teased mine open with his tongue. The crowd became nothing more than a muffled chatter far away, the heat rose—but this heat was different. It was pleasant heat. And then I had to push him away. I'd completely forgotten to breathe. I took a few breaths.

"Put me down," I said.

"Go ahead, tell me that was a bad idea."

"It *was* a bad idea."

"I wanted you to know what you're missing."

But I did kind of know what I was missing. And that in itself was enough reason to turn him down.

Now he went ahead and asked me, "Why? Why are you and I a bad idea?"

"You're a cop and I'm a—"

"A snoop who keeps sticking his nose where it doesn't belong."

I frowned at him. "A concerned citizen."

"And why shouldn't a cop and a concerned citizen go out on a date?"

"Don't you have rules against that?"

"No one pays attention to them."

"Well you should."

"Call the city council."

"I asked you to let go of me," I said, trying for firm.

He looked into my eyes for a long moment and then loosened his grip, allowing me to slide down his chest. I stepped back and stared at him.

"Why are you dressed like that? I thought you just came out?"

"Is there something wrong with my outfit?"

"No, that's the problem."

He shrugged. "I work in Silver Lake. I see how guys dress." That made more sense than I wanted it to. I could have mentioned that the kiss was not the kiss of a novice, but I knew that being in the closet didn't mean you never had sex. It just meant you lied about it.

I reminded myself that figuring him out didn't matter. I

wasn't going to get involved with him, so why he suddenly looked like a sex god wasn't important. In fact, I really needed to get away from him. Without so much as a "see you later" I turned and started walking toward Trunks.

I pushed my way through the throng on the sidewalk. The crowd had only grown since the parade began. People arriving late. I knew that Trunks was going to be packed. I wasn't going to just go in and quickly grab something from the bar, it was going to be an ordeal. I decided I'd order a couple of bottles of water and a Coke.

Inside, the bar was woody and dark and in the process of breaking all the fire codes. There had to be double the number of people they could legally accommodate. Though, to be honest, they'd have had to hire a phalanx of bouncers to keep people out. I squeezed my way toward the bar. When I got close enough, I saw that the bartender was filling plastic cups with ice and water to give away. I guessed he was trying to get some of the crowd to go back out and watch the parade.

I reached around the guy in front of me and grabbed a cup of water. I drank half of it right down. Then I decided to walk to the back and find the restroom. I'd swing by and get more water on my way out. I didn't have to go too badly, but knew I should. Who knew when my next opportunity might be?

Pushing through the throng took almost five minutes. When I got to the back I found there was a line of about ten guys. It was hot and muggy; the air conditioning must have given up an hour ago. I leaned against the wall. Across from me, on the other side of the bar, was a couple making out. The one guy was tall and blond and already had a terrible sunburn; the other was a short, stocky, probably Latino guy—

Oh my God! I was looking at Robert making out with his boss, Billy Martinez. I pushed away from the wall. Just then, they broke for a breather. Robert turned and looked at me. His eyes widened and he mouthed the word, "Shit."

Pushing my way through the seething crowd I got out of the bar as quickly as I could.

16

My theory in choosing a doctor was all about real estate. I assumed the better the doctor the more rent they'd be able to pay. Becker-Morse Medical Group was located in a pink granite building on Robertson just below Burton Way. A stone's throw from Beverly Hills. I was sure their offices were fabulously expensive.

My doctor was Dr. Morse—Dr. Sam, as he liked to be called. He was very attractive, naturally blond with blue eyes and pink skin. On the lapel of his thin white medical jacket was a red and blue Clinton/Gore button. I was pretty sure there had been some campaign brochures in the lobby too. He was all in for Clinton and started my appointment by asking, "You're registered to vote, right?"

"I am."

"Good boy." He smiled, apparently assuming that meant I was voting for Clinton. "How have things been going?"

"I passed out at a party," I confessed.

"Did you?" Dr. Sam opened my file and glanced at my most recent blood tests. "You're a little anemic. I can give you something for that."

"That's okay, I'll just try to eat more red meat."

"Sorry. That's not how this kind of anemia works."

Great. More drugs, I thought.

"How are you feeling otherwise?"

I shrugged. "Okay."

"Depressed?"

"No. Not really."

"It would be pretty normal if you were."

"Maybe a little." I said, just to be polite. A corpse in the courtyard certainly upped my stress level but it also kept me kind of engaged.

"Do you have anyone to talk to?"

"I have friends."

"Friends you can talk to about being HIV positive?"

I shrugged. "No one in particular."

"When you don't tell people what's going on with you, you're isolating yourself. Isolating yourself is bad for your health."

I had the distinct feeling he'd just been to a conference titled, "Depression and the HIV-positive Patient."

"I'm kind of a private person."

"I'm not suggesting you wear a sign, but one or two people you can talk to about how you feel would be a good thing."

I shrugged.

"Okay. Well, your tests look very good. Your T-cells are holding steady, which is what we were hoping to see. I'd like to see them climb a bit in the coming months. How are you tolerating the medication?"

"Well, I faint at parties."

"In addition to that…"

"I don't eat a lot. I feel kind of queasy most of the time."

"Okay, have you been avoiding spicy food, fried food and sweets?"

"Not really," I admitted. He'd just described most of my diet.

"That would be a start. Drink a lot of fluids: water, apple juice, soda—but let it go flat first. Ice is good, too. When it's hot out suck on an ice cube. It'll cool you off and settle your stomach at the same time."

Okay, that was unexpected. My doctor was prescribing ice.

A newspaper box was chained to a lamppost in front of Pinx, selling the *Los Angeles Times*. I almost never bought it; headlines are enough for me. I scanned them before I walked into the store. Apparently, the earthquakes were a much bigger deal than we'd thought while a quarter-million people lining Santa Monica Boulevard was not worth putting on the front page.

While I was standing there reading the front page for free and saving myself a whole quarter, Mikey stepped out of the store and said, "Um, Noah, there's this guy here. He's been waiting to see you for about an hour."

I walked into Pinx expecting that Lance Lavender had come back, but there was Robert looking like a lobster who'd managed to flop out of the pot. In addition to his sunburn, he wore a tight, striped T-shirt, and these pants he'd gotten at an Army surplus store that had extra sets of pockets. He had a half a dozen pairs and always wore them to work so he could keep scissors and tape measures and spools of thread and whatever else in the extra pockets. He also wore a long white scarf wrapped around his neck a half dozen times.

"I was wondering if we could talk," he said when he saw me.

I was pretty sure it was after one o'clock. "Are you on your lunch hour?"

"Yes, I stopped by your apartment first—"

"Have you had lunch?"

"We don't need to—"

"Mikey, we're going down to Taco Maria. Can I bring something back for you?"

"Yes, I'll have the taco combination with carne asada. And a Coke."

"Okay. I'll be back in half an hour or so." Then I looked at Robert and said, "Let's go."

As soon as we walked out of Pinx, he unwound the scarf and covered his head. He looked like a bizarrely tall Middle-

Eastern woman. He saw me looking at him and said, "What? I burned my scalp. It's very painful."

"I didn't think you were actually outside long enough to burn that bad."

"Believe it or not I saw almost the entire parade. All three hours. I think they'll let anyone in nowadays. I swear the final group was carrying a sign that said, 'I met a gay person once.'"

We walked into Taco Maria and took a booth. Then I went up to the counter and ordered our lunches, along with Mikey's to-go order. There's no actual waitress. When our lunches were ready the cook would bring them out.

We sat in the booth with our Cokes.

"What were you doing with Billy Martinez?"

"We're, you know, together."

"But—" I wanted to say it was entirely possible Billy was a murderer, because it was. Then I realized it was also entirely possible Robert was in on it and the only reason I wasn't considering that was that he used to be my friend.

"You know he's a suspect in Anthony Mercer's death."

"No, he's not. They arrested that kid who worked for him."

"Kerry didn't do it."

"So you think Billy did?" He shook his head. "Billy didn't kill Anthony. Trust me."

"Why? Why didn't Billy kill Anthony? You know he's trying to buy Mercy Costumes and he's been trying to buy it for a while."

"But he's not—" Robert stopped.

"What?"

"Billy and I were together the night Anthony was killed."

"Billy probably hired someone. The way Anthony was killed suggests it was a professional."

"Then why would they arrest Kerry? He's hardly a professional killer. He's hardly a professional anything."

That was an excellent point. I wished I'd thought of it when I was talking to Detective O'Shea. "What's the deal with you and Billy anyway? I thought you hated him."

"We're trying to keep our relationship under wraps."

"So you went to a bar on Santa Monica Boulevard and made out?"

"It was Trunks; who goes to Trunks?"

"You might have a point, but you obviously picked the wrong day. And why are you keeping your relationship under wraps? No one cares if you sleep with your boss."

"They might."

"Why?"

"I'm moving up. I've got my own Vegas show to design and we don't want it to look like Billy got me the job."

"Because Billy got you the job?"

"Of course he did. And I don't care if people know it. *After* the show opens, *after* it's a success. Then it won't matter."

"What's the show?"

"Wilma Wanderly at Lucky Days Casino."

I stared at him blankly for a moment. "So did you tell Wilma that Jeffer had a dress?"

"Yes, I did. It clinched the deal. I'm handling the lobby exhibit as well."

That was interesting. Bunny Hopper said she told Wilma. It was possible they both did. Apparently, everyone in L.A. knew Jeffer had the dress, except me.

Just then our food arrived, along with a bag containing Mikey's lunch.

Robert watched me intently. I wasn't sure why until he said, "Go ahead, take your pills."

I had been planning to take them when I got back to Pinx, but now I didn't need to wait. I took the wadded-up tissue out of my pocket. Opened it and took the pills quickly, one after another.

"I guess Tina can't keep a secret."

"No, she can't. But you know that already."

Actually, he was right. I should have remembered she was terrible at secrets. I'd ordered a chicken taco with no salsa, rice and beans. I picked up my fork but stopped when he said, "But Judith had already told me."

"Judith has been busy."

"She was trying to get information from me."

"What information?"

"How long you might live."

"Excuse me?"

"You know straight people, the minute you say someone's positive they're picking out flower arrangements for the funeral."

"Why does it matter to her—" And then it hit me like a glass of cold water in the face. "She's going to sue my estate for the dress?"

"Only if you die soon."

"I have no intention of dying soon," I said.

"Good, I'm glad to hear that."

And as though to prove my point, I then ate everything on my plate. While we ate, Robert made the occasional comment. Like, "I am actually in love with Billy. Believe it or not."

Since I thought Billy might be a murderer, congratulations didn't seem in order. I just smiled.

"The Wanderly show is going to be amazing."

"Isn't she a little, well…frail?" I said through a mouthful of rice.

"That's actually the best thing about it. It's like dressing a mannequin. I don't have to worry about how she'll be able to dance or even move. I mean, there will be dancers working around her, but they're easy. Sequins, Danskins, leotards—voila! She only has three changes. I mean she's talk-singing five or six songs and telling a few Hollywood stories. There will be some old photos projected behind her. The show's going to be forty-five minutes tops."

"And there will be memorabilia in the lobby," I said.

"Yes. Well, hopefully. We have a few things, but the crown jewel was going to be the dresses from *The Girl From Albany*."

"When did all this happen?" I asked, wiping my mouth with a paper napkin.

"It came together maybe a month ago."

"But, you said knowing about Jeffer's dress clinched the deal. Wilma was already negotiating to buy Anthony's dress."

"No, that's not possible."

"What do you mean?"

"I mean, Billy was negotiating to buy Mercy Costumes. The dress was part of the deal."

If that was true then Billy had no reason to kill Anthony.

And then I wondered about something. Something that might be important. When was Brick Masters going into Hollywood Costume for his fittings? And was it the same time Wilma Wanderly was there?

Walking into Pinx, I went right over to the counter to give Mikey his lunch.

"How much do I owe you?" he asked.

"Nothing. I just bought you lunch."

"You can't afford to buy me lunch."

"Yes, I can."

"No, you can't. I saw the letter you got from your insurance company on your desk."

"Oh, don't worry about that. I'm sure I'll work it out," I lied. I had no idea how I'd work it out.

"I just go to County/USC. It's fifty dollars a visit if you pay up front and that includes everything you need."

"Including hospitalization?"

"No, that's a different thing all together. I think you have to go on Medicaid for that. But the clinic's great."

I could use the clinic, it would certainly be cheaper—but would I get the same doctor each time I went? Would I get the same kind of care?

"Of course, you have to be prepared for the wait. One time it took me three hours to get in."

"No. That's not going to work."

I decided I'd better change the subject. "Listen, about the lube—" And wouldn't you know it, a woman who was clearly a mom walked up at just that moment. She was renting *The Little Mermaid* and *Beauty and the Beast*.

I stood there with my mouth shut while Mikey checked her

out. As soon as she walked out of the store, I said, "The thing is, it worked. Carl and Denny talked up the lube and it sold. So on the one hand you're right. But on the other hand, I don't think I'm wrong. Some of our customers could easily be offended. And if we lost just two or three regulars we could actually lose money on the lube."

Mikey thought that through. "Okay, you're right. We might offend people. I guess we have to come up with some kind of system for choosing—"

"I don't think that works, though. You really can't look at people and know whether they're interested in lube."

"If they're renting a porno—"

"Then I'm not worried about them. I'm worried about the people nearby."

"What about a flyer?" Mikey suggested.

"That we could put in the bag for anyone who rents porn. With a ten percent off coupon."

That was perfect. I'd gotten my way and Mikey had come up with a solution he could totally commit to. I was hugely relieved. I'd actually gotten something to work out.

I went back to my office and dialed information. I asked for Arthur Feldman's number in Burbank and wrote it down. Then I hung up and dialed.

"Arthur Feldman's office," a woman answered.

"May I speak to him? This is Noah Valentine."

"I'm afraid he's stepped away. Can I take a message?"

Stepped away? To where? Having been to his office, I couldn't image there were a lot of places he could step away to.

"I could wait, if he's not going to be long?"

"I'm sorry I don't know how long he's going to be."

"Do you know when he left?"

"No, I'm sorry. Would you like to leave a message?"

"But you sit—" And then I realized I was talking to an answering service and that's why she had no idea where he went or when he'd be coming back. He just flipped a switch or made a call or did something, and she started answering his phone.

"Thanks, I'll call back later," I said.

I hung up and wondered if there wasn't another way to find out if Brick Masters and Wilma Wanderly were ever in the same place at the same time. I couldn't think of one.

Putting that aside, I tried to turn my attention to my tax issues, only to end up taking a ninety-minute nap instead. I woke up at four twenty. Carl and Denny should already have arrived.

Then I wondered, did I ever give Mikey a break? I mean, I brought him lunch, but that's not the same as being able to walk around freely in the store and go to the bathroom or get a bottle of water.

Oh my God, I didn't. He should have said something. I went out front intending to send him home early, but when I got there everything was fine. Carl and Denny were taking over and Mikey was packing up.

"Noah, I told them about our idea to make a flyer," Mikey said. Which was nice of him to say, since it really had been his idea. "They think it's a great idea."

"Oh, good." And then I had to ask, "Do you guys watch soap operas?"

"We do. It gives me something to talk about with my mother," Carl said. "She's almost ninety, but she loves her stories."

"Do you watch *The Edge of Light*?"

"Yes, that's one of the better ones."

"Did it have a story line about a hostage situation?"

They both nodded.

"When was that?"

"It was sometime last month," Carl said.

"That story line ended around the fifteenth," Denny said.

"Well, now how do you know that?" Carl wanted to know.

"Darling, don't you remember? That was the day Shelly was in town, so we spent the day with her and put the machine on record."

"And then it missed the last five minutes."

"So we missed the shoot-out. It was devastating."

"Thanks, that's what I needed to know," I said and went back to my office.

Brick Masters could have met Wilma Wanderly around that time and she could have convinced him to go on the blind date with Anthony, distracting him long enough for someone to slip into the costume shop and steal the dress.

And so I was back to Wilma Wanderly.

17

Marc and Louis were still sitting in the courtyard when I got home around eight thirty. Their dinner dishes were cleared and they were having coffee along with snifters of brandy. Marc was enjoying a cigarette. I sat down with them and said, "It's definitely Wilma Wanderly."

"Really?" Louis said. "What makes you say that?"

"Billy Martinez was negotiating to buy Mercy Costumes, so he had no reason to kill Anthony. More importantly, Billy wanted the dress included in the deal."

"Why did he want the dress?" Marc asked.

"I thought about that a lot this afternoon," I said. "Robert didn't say so, but I think he and Billy were planning to get ahold of both dresses. One from Anthony, the other from me. Then they'd rent them to Wilma for the duration of her show, probably at about what she was willing to spend to buy them. After the show, after all the publicity, they'd auction them off."

"For a fortune," Louis added.

"Yes, I think so."

"So, they were planning to cheat Wilma?" Marc asked.

"I'm not sure that's called cheating," Louis said. "I think it's just called business."

"Either way, why not kill Billy? Or Robert?"

"Because it wouldn't have gotten her the dress. And that's what she wanted most."

"There's something else," I said. "I found out that Brick Masters was getting his costume fittings at Hollywood Costume around the time Wilma was in there arranging her new Las Vegas show."

"You really think she did it?" Louis asked.

"I do. Yes."

"Then we have to figure out who she used to do her dirty work."

"How would we do that?" Marc asked. "It could be anyone. She used to date mobsters. It could be some old friend."

"Or it could be her son," Louis replied.

"We could get her to confess," I suggested.

Could I get her to confess? I certainly wasn't having any luck figuring out who she'd hired. Suddenly, it occurred to me, "Brick knew who the killer was."

"Yes, that's probably what got him killed," Louis agreed.

"So if I tell her I can connect her to Brick, maybe she'll confess."

"Or have you killed."

"It takes time to arrange a murder, though," I said.

"Unless the hired gun is her son," Marc repeated.

"I don't think it's her son. She barely trusts him making a phone call. I don't think she'd trust him with something like this."

"But even if you do get her to confess, it's just hearsay," Marc said.

"How do you know that?" Louis asked.

"It was on *L.A. Law*. You'd already fallen asleep."

"What you need to do is a sting." Louis said. "You know, like they did to DeLorean."

"You mean record it?"

"Yeah, that's what I mean."

"So I just arrive at her house with a video crew?" I said, sarcastically.

"Given that she's a movie star, that might actually work," Marc said.

"You could also just put a tape recorder in your pocket," Louis said. "You can find them that small."

But how would I get her to confess? I asked myself. I couldn't just call her up and say I wanted to come over and take her confession. The meeting would have to be about—

Then I had an idea. "I could tell her I have the dress she wants. And that I'm ready to sell it to her."

"And then?" Louis asked.

"And then I tell her I can connect her to Brick. And that I won't sell her the dress unless I know the truth about what happened to him."

They sat there considering. Louis swirled his brandy around and took a sip. He looked at Marc and said, "We should go with him."

"No. She'll never confess if there are three of us," I insisted.

"We could at least sit in the car," Marc said.

"That's not going to do any good. I mean, we're just getting a regular tape recorder, right? We're not getting some van with headphones and a reel-to-reel."

"He's right," Louis said. "Anything could happen and we'd have no idea."

We chatted over a few other details and then I went upstairs to make the phone call. It was a little after nine. Before I could lose my nerve, I found Wilma Wanderly's card and dialed her number.

"Miss Wanderly?" I asked when a woman answered.

"Yes."

"This is Noah Valentine. I have the dress and I'm ready to make a deal."

"Marvelous. Can you bring it now?"

That threw me. I wasn't even close to being ready. "No, I can't. I can bring it tomorrow night. Around seven."

"Excellent. I'll be here."

Tuesdays were not the busiest day of the week at Pinx, so I didn't feel too bad calling Mikey and telling him I might not be in at all.

"Are you sick? You looked a little pale yesterday."

Reflexively, I wanted to say I was fine, but that would just worry him more. "I'm a little under the weather."

"Get some rest. Do you want me to drop off some videos when my shift ends?"

That was right about the time I expected to be on my way to Wilma Wanderly's. "No, that's all right. I'm hoping to sleep most of the day."

After I hung up, I went down and stood at the corner waiting for Louis to pick me up. It was about eleven thirty. He'd told his boss he had a doctor's appointment so he'd be taking a long lunch. He swung by right on time and we drove about ten blocks.

Eye Spy was hardly a subtle kind of shop. Located on Sunset Boulevard just before you crossed over into Echo Park, it had big signs across the front of its shack-like building proclaiming HIDDEN CAMERAS, COVERT AUDIO and SPY GEAR. Louis pulled his Honda up in front.

We got out of the car, squinting into the sunlight, Louis fed the meter, and we walked into the store. Inside, the store was tiny. Half the place was taken up by an L-shaped display case. On the wall behind the case hung a sign that offered to take care of all your surveillance needs. I guessed that was probably how they stayed in business; selling security cameras like the one at Mercy Costumes.

A man sat on a stool behind the counter. He was in his early fifties, thin and dried out. He wore a hunter's ammo vest that was green and had two rows of finger-sized pockets to slip rifle rounds into. They were all full. He had a Bush/Quayle button stuck into the vest alongside a nametag that said, BUCK.

"Good afternoon," Buck said.

We smiled at him.

Louis cut to the chase. "We're looking for a concealable recording device. Something that could easily fit into a pocket."

He got off the stool and led us down to the far end of the case. In front of us was a collection of listening devices. Gadgets you could attach to a telephone, complicated systems of small bugs that could transmit and clunky tape recorders that received, and the micro recorders we were looking for. He reached into the case and pulled out a square recorder that was only a tiny bit bigger than the microcassette it recorded onto.

"This is the simplest and most reliable recorder. Just put it into your pocket. It's voice activated. As soon as you or whoever starts talking it starts recording."

I glanced at the price tag and then pulled Louis a step away. "It's almost five hundred dollars," I whispered into his ear.

He nodded. "Yes, I saw that."

Turning back to Buck he asked, "Do you have one that you rent?"

"Twenty-five dollars a day. And you have to buy your own microcassettes. If you want the microcassettes transferred onto regular cassettes I can do that for ten dollars a tape."

Well, that was certainly more affordable than five hundred dollars. Not to mention, I really didn't expect to ever use it again. Louis told Buck we'd take it for one day. Then he turned to me and asked, "What about a Taser? Might come in handy."

I glanced at the case. Tasers ran from around a hundred to five hundred dollars. I could rent one but—

"I don't need a Taser to go see an old lady."

"An old lady who's responsible for two deaths. I'd rethink that." Louis turned to Buck and asked, "You rent Tasers too, don't you?"

"I do."

"We'll take the easiest one to operate."

"They're all pretty easy."

"Small," I said. Then I looked at Louis and said, "It has to go in a pocket just like the tape recorder."

Louis dropped me off at home about an hour and a half later.

We'd had lunch at a sandwich shop in a strip mall on Sunset a few blocks from Eye Spy called Loretta's. There was a billboard in the corner of the parking lot for *Batman Returns*. Louis had wanted Mexican, but I asked for something bland since I'd had Mexican the day before.

"I can't believe places like that exist," I said, taking a bite of my turkey and Swiss on white bread. "Is all of that stuff legal?"

"Legal to sell," he said. "I'm not sure how legal it is to use."

"Is what I'm doing illegal?"

"Not sure. But I think as long as she confesses to murder, you'll be fine."

"How did you find that place?"

"Just drove by it. It's not the kind of place you forget."

I was a little nervous about our sting, but I didn't want to say so. I must have had a funky look on my face because Louis said, "You don't have to do this, you know."

"What happens if I don't, though? That poor kid stays in jail."

"You only met him once," Louis pointed out.

"I know."

"And he's only been arrested. If he has a good attorney—"

"Who's going to get him a good attorney?"

"Good question."

When I walked into my apartment the first thing I noticed was the fabric pulled off my love seat and the original, dirty white velour showing. It was also turned onto its back, the material covering the bottom ripped out. The armoire was open, the CDs and VHS tapes had been pulled out into a pile in front of the armoire. I turned to my left and saw that my desk drawers were open, and the contents of the center drawer dumped onto the desktop. I took a few steps in that direction and saw the kitchen cabinets were also all opened.

I set the package from Eye Spy onto my table and went into the bedroom. Every one of the built-in cupboards was open. The closets were both emptied and my clothes piled on the floor. The storage boxes I kept under the bed had been pulled out and dumped onto the bed.

Whoever had been here was looking for the dress. That was pretty obvious. When they didn't find it, they must have begun looking for a key, or even the location of the lockup where the dress might be. Rifling through my underwear drawer, my desk drawer, the box where I kept silly things like a pair of cufflinks my dad wore and my class ring.

Going back into the living room, I looked around for the phone, which was off its base. It took a few minutes, but I eventually found it underneath a sofa cushion. I didn't call 911. I called information instead and asked for Rampart Station. When I was given the number I agreed to pay the extra twenty-five cents to have them connect me.

I asked for Detective O'Shea and was put on hold. Three minutes later the phone was picked up and a woman's voice said, "Detective Wellesley."

"Oh, hello, I'm calling for Detective O'Shea. This is Noah Valentine."

"Detective O'Shea isn't available right now. What can I do for you?"

"Someone has broken into my apartment and ransacked it. They were searching for something."

"Money," Wellesley said. "It was probably addicts. They break in and search for cash. Did they take any of your CDs?"

"No. They didn't take anything."

"Keep checking. I'm sure they took something. I can be there in about a half an hour."

"Do you remember the address?"

"Yes, I remember the address. And I remember you."

The way she said the last sentence wasn't all that cordial.

I waited in the courtyard, sitting at the table where we had dinner each week, for nearly an hour before Detective Wellesley showed up. When she arrived, she arrived alone. That was annoying. I would have liked to see Detective O'Shea or at least someone from SID. They could have collected fingerprints, at least.

Wellesley said "Hey," and then we walked up the stairs to

the second floor. "Do you have any idea what they were looking for?"

"Yes, a blue spangled dress. Whoever did this killed Anthony Mercer and Brick Masters."

"Uh, no. We have Anthony's killer in custody."

"Then why would someone break into my apartment and go through my things?"

She ignored my question. "How did they get in?"

"I'm not sure. Probably through one of the windows."

She glanced at them. The screens were on, but they were all open. She scowled at me and asked, "You leave them open like that?"

"It gets stuffy if I don't." That was embarrassing. I sounded like a princess.

"You should ask your landlord for security bars."

It was the second time this year someone had gotten into my apartment; bars weren't a bad idea. Of course, I was pretty sure neither break-in was random. I'd never felt unsafe because a random thief had to walk by most of the other apartments in the building to get to mine, which was also the most visible. A random burglar would pick someone else long before they got to me.

"Which window?" she wanted to know.

"I don't know. Whoever it was put the screen back on."

She gave me a 'You're kidding me' look. I shrugged. Then she opened the door and walked into my apartment. She wasn't wearing gloves and that annoyed me a little. It made me feel like she wasn't taking this seriously.

"Do you have a lot of old boyfriends?" she asked.

"No."

"Really? No?"

"I had a partner for about five years. He died last year." And that was somehow more embarrassing than not keeping my windows shut because it got stuffy.

She looked around at the mess. "And nothing was taken?"

"No. I said that already."

"You like Detective O'Shea, don't you?"

"He's okay."

"You asked for him when you called."

"So?"

"So, are you disappointed he didn't come?" That was a question I didn't dare answer. Of course I was disappointed he hadn't come. She was rude and didn't seem to be doing her job.

"You think I did this myself? Is that what you're saying to me?"

"I'm not saying anything. I'm asking questions. Nothing is missing?"

"I don't think so."

She shrugged. "Like I said on the phone, it was most likely a drug addict, crack, crank, whatever's popular. They break in, steal your CDs, your videotapes, then sell them to some place like Rockaway Records."

"My CDs are all there."

She glanced at the pile on the floor and asked, "How will you know until you put them away?"

I didn't have a good answer to that.

"You should get someone out here to look for fingerprints," I said.

"I'm afraid we have limited resources. I'm not sure I can justify it if nothing was taken."

After Wellesley left it was still early, but I decided to get ready anyway. I took another shower, tried to do something creative with my hair—always time consuming—and then asked myself the important question, *What do you wear to a sting*? Were some colors more conducive to eliciting confessions? Green? Blue? I had no idea. The only thing I did know was that I needed big pockets.

I stood staring at my clothes on the floor, wondering what I should wear. I probably should have just put everything back into the closet, but I wasn't all that focused. I grabbed a pair of baggy houndstooth check pants from the pile. They were loose in the thighs and hips, and cuffed at the ankle. A bit formal, perhaps, but I was going to see a movie star. Maybe they were just fine. I put them on and then got the recorder from the living room, and slipped it into the front pocket. It was unnoticeable.

Then I put the Taser gun into the other pocket. It was bigger, so it was more noticeable. That told me I had to pick the right shirt. I had a black short-sleeved shirt, rayon and too big for me. It would hang down over the pockets and hide the Taser. I slipped into my Docs, avoided looking at my hair since it was probably already doing something annoying, and spritzed on a little Antaeus. I was ready to go.

All I had to do was wait two and a half hours.

18

"DID YOU BRING THE DRESS?" WILMA SAID, AFTER SHE LET me in.

"Of course not. Someone broke into my apartment this afternoon trying to steal it." I was nervous and jittery and had imagined this playing out a hundred different ways.

"Well, it certainly wasn't me."

"Wasn't it? I told you I had the dress and then my apartment got ransacked. I'd say there's a connection."

We walked into her living room. The marble floor made it feel particularly chilly even though the sun hadn't set and it was probably in the high seventies. Albert sat on one of the sofas with stacks of envelopes in front of him. He was putting the same letter in each one, then licking the envelopes.

"Albert, Albert, use the sponge. You're going to get a paper cut on your tongue." It was the most maternal thing I'd heard her say to him, but then she had to add, "I don't want you bleeding on the envelopes."

She arranged herself on the sofa, saying, "It's newsletter time. Once a month. My fan club just adores hearing from me. Well, actually they hear from Albert. Don't tell! Now, where were we...oh yes, you accused me of trying to steal your dress."

"Someone tried to steal it."

"Why would I steal something I'm perfectly willing to pay for?" Then to Albert she added, "He didn't bring the dress. I can't believe it's this difficult to spend a lot of money on an old dress."

"He doesn't have it. I told you he didn't have it."

"He said he has it, so he has it. You have it, don't you?"

"I do."

To Albert she said, "See? He just doesn't trust us. Probably thinks we're going to take it from him at gunpoint." Looking me up and down, she said, "I imagine you'll want to make the exchange in a public place. Are you willing to take a check or do I have to stuff cash in an old duffle bag?"

Albert ignored his mother's request and licked an envelope.

"What kind of a deal did you make with Brick Masters?" I asked.

"Ouch," Albert said, cutting his tongue.

"See, I told you you'd get a paper cut. Why won't you ever do what I say? What kind of a deal did I make with whom?"

"Brick Masters."

"I don't know who that is."

"Oh, I think you do. You met him at Hollywood Costume. He was there for a fitting. He had a job on *The Edge of Light*. You set him up on a date with Anthony so that he could leave the door—"

She looked at her son, "Albert? Is he talking about that very pretty boy you were trying to pick up?"

"I wasn't trying to pick him up, Mother. I'm not gay. How many times do I have to tell you that?"

"It's all right, dear. You know I love the sissy boys and the sissy boys love me."

"You were talking to Brick?" I asked Albert. "Did you try to steal the dress for your mother?"

He laughed. Then his hand flew up to his mouth to cover.

"Why is that funny?" I asked.

"No reason."

"You did steal the dress for your mother, didn't you?"

He laughed again. "Shit."

"Albert, you know I hate it when you're obtuse."

Ignoring her, he said to me, "It's funny that you think I'd steal the dress *for* her."

"What kind of thing is that to say?" Wilma asked. "Of course you'd steal the dress for me. You're my devoted son."

"Am I, Mother?"

He picked up another envelope and licked it.

"Albert! Use the sponge."

"Shut up."

"What did you say?"

"I said, shut up." Then he got up abruptly, managed to knock a box of stuffed envelopes onto the floor and pulled a gun on us.

"Albert, you've got a gun."

"Yes, Mother, I've got a gun."

"Well, you look ridiculous. Put it away, this instant."

He turned to me and smiled—or rather his lips curled into something resembling a smile. "I was only trying to steal the dress from Anthony, honest. I'd tried breaking in a couple weeks before, but the alarm went off and I couldn't risk it. I knew that would just make things harder, so I arranged for Ford Wheeler to set up the date with Brick. He was supposed to keep Anthony distracted while I got into the building. I planned to wait there until they were gone and take my time looking for the dress.

"But it didn't work out that way. Anthony was suspicious. Brick was very good-looking and he couldn't see why Ford would set him up with a guy that attractive. He started asking questions. Questions Brick wasn't very good at answering. He was the kind of actor who needed a script. And even then...

"Once, I was in the building I heard them arguing. And then I heard Brick say my name. I snuck over to the work area and listened to enough of the conversation to know it was all over. I still wanted the dress, though, so I stepped out into the open, made Anthony get on his knees, and shot him in the back of the head. Just the way Gianni Agnotti told me they did it."

"Oh Gianni, he was such a nice man," Wilma said.

"He was a mobster," her son replied.

"He was a *nice* mobster!"

"You wanted to find that dress for me. Dear, that's so sweet, but I already had a deal with Anthony—"

Albert burst into laughter. "I wasn't trying to get the dress *for* you! No. No. I was trying to steal the dress from Anthony *before* he could sell it to the great Miss Wanderly. I wouldn't kill anyone for you. Oh, I would kill people; I *did* kill people, but I did it to stop you. You wanted that fucking dress more than anything in the world and I was going to make sure you didn't get it."

"Albert, how could you?" Wilma said.

"How could I? After the way you've treated me my whole life? Like I was a lackey, a flunky, a gofer. The personal assistant you gave birth to. How could I not, Mother?"

"But Albert, I've never done anything but love you." She said it like it was a line in a movie. I don't think any of us were convinced.

"You never loved me," he said. "I wasn't attractive. I wasn't talented. In your world that meant I was nothing but a big flop. I was a disappointment." Turning to me he continued, "Do you know she sent me away to boarding school so she didn't have to look at me? That's how big a disappointment I was. But the problem is, children don't stay at boarding school forever. Do they Mother?"

"I thought it would be good for you, that you'd come back…better."

"Yeah, well, I came back. There was talk of sending me away to college, but I didn't want to go. So I made myself useful. Indispensable. Eventually, she started to say that, 'Birthing her own personal assistant was the smartest thing she ever did.' Do you remember that, Mother? I knew then she'd never send me away."

"What about Brick Masters? Why did you kill him?"

"I didn't have any choice. When Lavender came back and told us you knew who'd killed Anthony, he started freaking out, talking about how it might be better to confess, that we'd get less time. Of course, *he* could say something like that. He'd only aided and abetted. I was the one who'd made Anthony—"

"So you killed him, too."

"Yes."

"What about Lavender? He was an actor, too, wasn't he?"

"No, he was really a collector."

"Is he dead?"

"Probably. I shot him three times. He just wouldn't get down on his knees."

"Darling, you can't keep shooting people. It's just not—"

"Good for your image? Well, it's good for mine. I'm going to be famous. I'm going to be a famous murderer. A famous *mass* murderer. What do you think of that, Mommy?"

"I suppose you're going to kill me next?" Wilma guessed.

"Why would I kill you? I could have killed you any time I felt like it. You're a heavy enough sleeper and you have all those ridiculous pillows on your bed. No, I want you to suffer. I want you to live as long as you can as the mother of a vile murderer." Then he turned the gun on himself, holding it up to his temple. "My next victim is me."

Wilma let out a little squeak.

"You don't want to do that, Albert," I said, my mind racing. "If you're dead, she can make up any story she wants about you. She could even say you're adopted and that you don't really have anything to do with her."

He was frowning. I must have been moving in the right direction. The gun in his hand began drooping.

"Won't it be worse for your mother if you were in jail? Where you could give interviews? Where you could tell people your side of the story?" As I spoke, I took a step toward him, slipping my hand into my pocket.

"You're right. I would be more trouble in prison, wouldn't I?"

"Good, why don't you put the gun down…?" I suggested. I had a firm grasp on the Taser just in case.

"But then there's no reason not to shoot a few more people. You, for instance. You're annoy—"

He raised the gun, but it was too late. I pushed the Taser into the side of his neck just like the instructions that came in the box had said to. He wobbled a few times and fell to the ground. As he did, the gun dropped out of his hand and hit the marble floor. It went off and a plate glass window shattered.

I was stunned. Shocked by what I'd done and even more shocked when Wilma walked over to slap me on the face, hard.

"How dare you? Why can't you just mind your own business?"

It wasn't the usual reaction you get from a mother when you save her son's life. But then, it was pretty clear Wilma was not your typical mother.

And then, unexpectedly, Detective O'Shea rushed into the room, gun drawn. Wellesley was with him in addition to a couple uniformed officers.

"Officer! Arrest this man!" Wilma screamed, pointing at me. "He came in here and attacked my son with that, that electrical thing."

Albert groaned from the floor.

I took the recorder out of my pocket and offered it to O'Shea. "Everything you need is on here."

And then I felt a little woozy. So I sat down right there on the floor.

19

LOUIS HAD DECORATED THE TABLE IN MINIATURE American flags and miniature rainbow flags. Marc had made the tablecloth from red, white and blue bandanas. It was Fourth of July that Saturday. Pinx was closed, and we didn't reopen until Monday morning.

When I got downstairs, Marc came out of their apartment and handed me a drink in a wine glass. I stared at it. It was very colorful.

"What is this?"

"It's a white wine berry sangria. White wine, 7-Up, strawberries, blueberries, lemon sherbet and a lot of ice."

I took a sip. It was sweet but good. But I shouldn't have it. It wasn't good for me. I took another sip anyway.

"There was another story in the paper this morning about Albert Wanderly," Marc said. "And an enormous sidebar all about his mother's career."

"She must be thrilled." That's when I noticed something. "There are five chairs. Who's coming to dinner?"

"Well, Leon of course, and a mystery guest."

"I think I've had my fill of mysteries," I said. The idea of another guest made me grumpy. When I'd first started having dinner with them, Marc and Louis had tried to fix me up a few times. I really hoped they weren't back to that.

"This mystery will get solved in the next few minutes. Don't worry."

Upstairs, my phone started to ring. I could have let the answering machine pick it up, but I was too curious. I set down my drink and ran upstairs. I snatched the phone off its cradle just before the answering machine would have answered.

"Hello?"

"Well, I've had it with Carolyn Harvey. I'm done with her."

"Hi, Mom. Isn't it getting late there?"

"I'm sorry. I just can't sleep after what happened."

I was going to have to ask, so I went ahead, "What happened?"

"You know I volunteer for the cancer society in honor of Jeffer. I told Carolyn that and she laughed at me. She said I was a fool to believe that a gay man of Jeffer's age died of anything but AIDS. Well, I told her you weren't like that. That you wouldn't lie to me. And then I walked out of the restaurant. We're done. I'm not having anything else to do with her."

For a moment my mouth went dry and I couldn't breathe. I had to say something, though. "You know, Mom, sometimes people lie to be kind."

She was quiet a long time, then she said, "It's true, then? Jeffer died of AIDS?"

"Yes, he did."

"And does that mean you…?"

"Yes. I'm HIV positive."

She went quiet again. I almost asked if she was still there, but I could hear her breathing. Finally she said, "I should have known, shouldn't I? I should have been able to figure this out on my own. Carolyn was right. I am a fool."

"Mom, just because Carolyn is accurate doesn't make her right. She wasn't being kind. For one thing, it's not her business, and for another if she really felt you needed to know she could have explained it in a much gentler way."

"She did seem almost happy about the whole thing."

"Some people enjoy being mean."

"Are you all right, Noah? If you're not...you'd tell me if...oh dear..."

She was close to tears and I did not want her to start crying.

"I'm fine Mom. My doctor is very happy with my progress. I'm taking the right meds and I've got insurance." *At least this month,* I thought. "Everything is as good as it can be."

"It's just that it all happened so fast with Jeffer. The same thing won't—"

"He'd had it for a long time and he wasn't taking care of himself. It seemed like it all happened very fast, but it really didn't."

I didn't want to talk about Jeffer too much. There were still things I didn't feel she needed to know. Like how exactly I'd gotten the virus.

"Do you want to go now? Do you want some time to think about this?"

"Oh no, no, not yet." She took a deep breath and got hold of herself. "I guess this is important. I'm not really sure, it sounded important but maybe it's not."

"What, what is it?"

"There's something I have to tell you. It all seemed kind of silly, at the time. Very cloak and dagger."

"Mom."

"All right. Well, Jeffer told me that someday you'd tell me a secret, and you did, you just told me a secret, didn't you? And when you told me that secret I was to give you the key."

"The key to what?"

"The lockup he had."

"You know about that? You have the key?"

"Yes, Noah, that's what I just said."

"Wait. Have you been paying for the storage since Jeffer died?"

"Yes. I mean, no. He's been paying. He sent me a big envelope full of cash one time and I've been using that."

"Do you know what's in the lockup?"

"No, I don't. I've been dying of curiosity. What's in it?"

"You kept this secret from me ever since Jeffer died? I can't believe you'd—"

"Don't get annoyed with me. You've been keeping a pretty big secret yourself."

That was unfortunately true.

We chatted a few more minutes. She promised to send me the key and told me she loved me. Afterward I took a few minutes to pull myself together. That phone call had been a lot to absorb and I wasn't sure I was doing a good job. My mother knew what was going on with me. She seemed to take it well. I was sure she'd have questions, but I figured the worst was over.

The whole thing with Jeffer and the lockup was harder to take in. What was he thinking? Why hadn't he ever told me about the lockup? Why hadn't he left me the key directly? And why make my mother wait to give it to me until I told her a secret?

He did know I hadn't told her I was HIV positive. Had he not wanted me to have what was in the locker until I was so sick I couldn't hide it from my mother anymore? She was almost three thousand miles away, it wasn't that hard to keep a secret from her. I might never have told her.

When I finally went back down to the courtyard, Leon was there, as well as the mystery guest. Detective O'Shea stood there with a glass of sangria in his hand. He was carefully dressed in pressed jeans, loafers without socks and a bright, white polo shirt that made his skin look very dark. The sun was on the verge of setting and it cast an almost magical glow over O'Shea. Well, it cast a glow over all of us; I only noticed it on the detective.

Staring at the table, Leon said, "Marc, you've made a complete mishmash of the hanky code. I have no idea what you want to do and/or have done to you."

"Good," Marc said. "I prefer it that way."

"What's the hanky code?" O'Shea asked.

"Oh my God," Leon exclaimed. "There ought to be a class. Introduction to Gayness."

"The hanky code is something from the late seventies,"

Louis explained, picking up a plate of pigs in a blanket and handing them around. "Guys used to go to bars with a colored bandana in their back pocket, which advertised what they wanted to do in bed. Some of them were very obvious. Like yellow meant you wanted water sports. Or brown if you—"

"Louis, that's enough," Marc said. "We're about to have dinner."

O'Shea was blushing. He'd gotten himself in much deeper than he liked. I decided to rescue him by asking, "So you found Lance Lavender's body?"

"We did. Shot three times. Just like Albert told you."

"Oh, that reminds me," Leon said. "I got a call from Ford Wheeler. He admitted setting up the date between Anthony and Brick. He's terrified he'll lose his career over this."

"Wellesley wants to charge him with obstruction," O'Shea said.

"Why didn't he come forward and say anything?" Marc asked.

"He didn't want to get involved. He says he wasn't sure Albert had done anything in one breath and then in the next he says he was terrified that Albert might kill him."

"Oh my Lordy," Louis said. "What a pickle."

"But why did he do it at all?" I asked. "Wasn't he suspicious?"

"Very. Apparently, Albert has something very juicy on him," Leon said.

"Well, it can't be sex, he's hardly discreet," Marc said. "You should have heard some of the things he said at the brunch."

"If it's not sex," O'Shea said. "Then it has to be money. It's always one or the other."

"That's not true," I pointed out. "You thought Kerry killed Anthony for revenge. And while we're on the subject, how could you think that poor kid killed two people?"

"Now that it's over, I can say this. I was never completely convinced. Wellesley is the one who rammed that through. And she was lead on the investigation."

"What about the gun?" I asked. "Willow said you found it the second time you searched Mercy Costumes."

"Albert left the gun hidden at the scene of the crime. Kerry found it and took it home. When the newspapers didn't mention the gun, Albert called in an anonymous tip."

"Why did he want you to find the gun?"

"He had a collection of guns he'd gotten from one of the mobsters his mother dated. They were all unregistered. He used one to kill Anthony and another to kill Brick. I think he hoped the guns would confuse us or set us off the track. And as it turns out, he was right."

"You know, come to think of it," Louis said. "The whole thing *was* about revenge."

"Or hatred," I suggested.

"Albert had major mommy issues," Leon said.

The previous Wednesday, Wilma Wanderly had done an interview on *Tonight's Entertainment News*. Mikey had insisted on playing the TV all day at Pinx, which meant the promos for the interview kept coming on. She began the interview trying to be rational and apologetic, and by the end she was sobbing. At one point she even said, "And the worst part is, now I have to hire an assistant." The interviewer and crew all gasped. Wilma quickly followed up with, "Oh what am I saying? I'm practically delirious with grief."

A bit later, Louis brought out a platter of bacon burgers and a huge bowl of potato salad. Marc followed with a tray of condiments for the burgers and a tomato mozzarella salad. For dessert we had an apple cranberry pie, since so many things were as American as apple pie. I didn't know of anything that was as American as cranberries, but Louis had a habit of 'perking' up his recipes with an extra ingredient or two.

I said goodnight around nine thirty. It was still early and I saw a hurt look flash across Javier's face. *Why was he being so persistent?* I wondered. Yes, the kiss was nice and I had returned it, but then I put my foot down and put an end to that. So why was he mooning over me?

I was almost curt in my goodbyes, but I wanted to get away

before Javier had a chance to chase after me. I was at the bottom of the stairs to the second floor when a hand stopped me. I turned around and saw Louis standing there. I was so relieved.

"I have something for you," he said, keeping his voice low. I was expecting a plate of hamburgers and potato salad, but his hands were empty. Glancing back at Javier, who was chatting with Marc, Louis reached into his pocket and pulled out a black film canister with a gray lid and a pack of rolling papers. "I assume you know how to roll a joint."

"I went to high school."

"It helps. With appetite. And nausea."

"Thanks," I said, quickly taking the canister and papers, and shoving them in a pocket.

When I got into my apartment, I locked the door and turned off all of the lights. I sat on my love seat and waited. The windows were open and I could hear that dinner was breaking up downstairs. Leon yawned loudly and announced he was leaving. I didn't hear Javier leave, but I knew he was gone when Marc and Louis began taking everything inside. They chatted a little but I couldn't hear what they were saying. I might have been able to if I sat on the other side of the apartment, but I didn't think it mattered what they were saying. They put out the Tiki torches and then there was nothing to light the courtyard.

I could have gone to bed, but something kept me sitting there. A few minutes later, I heard someone quietly coming up the steps to the second floor then just as softly come down to my door. He tapped on my door. Then waited, and tapped again.

"Noah," Javier said quietly. "Are you awake?"

I sat in the darkness and said nothing.

The key arrived on the morning of the eighth. My mother wasn't able to send it until Monday the sixth. When I called to thank her, she said, "We never talked about Wilma Wanderly. It just seems so odd to me that you met her one week and the next she's all over the papers. Well, her son is. I can't imagine having a child who'd get involved with something like that."

"Mom, he wasn't 'involved,' he murdered people. Three, in fact."

I decided against telling her I was in any way connected with Albert's capture, telling myself she had enough to deal with learning that I was HIV positive. There was no need to mention that someone had recently held a gun on me.

The storage facility was the one on Beverly Boulevard near Virgil, the old Deco building that was about fifteen stories tall. Robert and Tina decided they just had to go with me, and so we went down around sunset. We parked on the street right in front since the meters stopped at six and were now free.

The building was light beige stone and ornately carved on the first floor. We walked around it until we found the entrance to the front desk. A sullen young man, practically a teenager, directed us to the elevators. I didn't even have to ask where Jeffer's lockup was, since the key itself gave me that information: 1117. We took the elevator to the eleventh floor.

"There's something I don't understand and you might know the answer, Robert."

"Oh God, this is one of those conversations," Robert said.

"Shush," Tina replied. "Noah deserves answers."

"Jeffer kept the storage unit a secret from me. He kept the dress a secret from me. Why did he do that?"

"Oh my God, I don't know," Robert said. "Seriously Noah, he didn't explain himself to me anymore than he did to you."

"He sent my mother the key with instructions so, obviously, he wanted me to have it so why not just tell me?"

"He knew what his family was like. Maybe he was trying to protect you," Tina suggested.

"But that's what the will was for."

"Yes, but that didn't work out the way he wanted, did it?"

"It might have, if we'd gone to court."

"And spent most of the estate on attorney fees."

"Look," Robert said. "It's hard to understand Jeffer. He did bad things. And he did good things. You just have to accept that this is one of the good things he did. He did worry about what would happen to you. You know, after."

He worried about me. Was that all it was? A secret rainy-day fund? I wouldn't have been able to keep the house. Not on what I made from Pinx. Did he think I'd foolishly try to live there again? Did he think I'd end up sick and penniless? Is that why he had my mother—

The elevator opened and we got out. In stark contrast to the outside of the building, the hallways were bland and unadorned.

"Is Wilma's show still happening?" I asked Robert.

"Of course it is. She had her agent renegotiate her contract. She's getting half a million more. She says she's going to use it to defend her son, but I'll believe that when I see it."

"I think he'll take a plea bargain," I said. "He's not going to give his mother the opportunity to sit bravely behind him in a courtroom. Or worse, talk to the press on the courthouse steps every day."

When we found the lockup, I squatted down and put the key in the lock. It popped open. Then I rolled up the door and the three of us stood there a moment taking in the small ten by ten-foot wide lockup. There were two rolling clothes racks full of costumes, a stack of boxes at the back, two steamer trunks and a half a dozen bags.

"Where did he get all of this?" I wondered out loud.

The first place I went was to the rack of clothing. I flipped through looking for—the blue dress. And, just as expected, it was there. I pulled it out and just looked at it for a few minutes.

Along the back collar, a seamstress had sewn in a hand-written tag that said, WILMA WANDERLY. The dress was tiny, almost child-sized. So much smaller than the one Wilma had shown me. Its lining had been white, but now it was dingy beige, almost tea-stained. The sequins were still vibrant and shimmering.

As I looked at that, Robert said, "We might be able to restore the lining. The lining could also be replaced without damaging the value too much."

"No, I think I'll sell it with Wilma's sweat intact."

I knew I should put the dress down and investigate the rest of the lockup, but I couldn't. The dress was an incredible piece of Hollywood memorabilia. It had also cost three men their lives and one man his freedom.

The blue dress meant different things to different people: to Wilma it had meant her comeback, to Bunny Hopper it was the dream of who she wanted to be, to Albert it meant revenge. I would be selling the dress. Wilma had offered me twenty-five thousand; I had a feeling I could get her up to at least thirty-six. Thirty-six thousand dollars was three years of health insurance.

For me, the dress meant life.

LOUIS' FOURTH OF JULY SANGRIA

- Several bottles of cheap white wine
- 1 liter 7-UP
- lemon sherbet
- pint of strawberries
- pint of blueberries

Combine wine and 7-UP in a large, very large, pitcher. Clean fruit. Remove stems. Slice strawberries. Add fruit to pitcher. Scoop sherbet into pitcher and stir. Serve immediately.

You may add a pint of vodka if it's that kind of party.

LOUIS' SUPER SIMPLE APPLE PIE

You'll need pie crust, enough for top and bottom. Use whatever recipe works best for you or purchase premade at the Mayfair.

- 6 cups of apples
- 1 cup dried cranberries
- ½ cup sugar
- 2 teaspoons cinnamon
- ¼ teaspoon nutmeg
- 4 tablespoons butter

For the apples, you can mix and match types. It's best with a couple of Macintosh, a couple of Granny Smiths and a Delicious. Peel and slice the apples into thin wedges. In a large bowl, combine the apples, cranberries, sugar and spices. Stir.

Line the pie pan with half of the crust. Pour in the filling. Dot the filling with butter. Use the other half of the crust on top and pinch the edges to seal the pie. Using a fork to create little holes for steam to escape during the baking.

Bake for 20 minutes at 400. Turn the oven down to 350 and continue to bake for 30-35 minutes, or until crust is golden and apple filling is bubbly.

ALSO BY MARSHALL THORNTON

The Perils of Praline

Desert Run

Full Release

The Ghost Slept Over

My Favorite Uncle

Femme

Praline Goes to Washington

Aunt Belle's Time Travel & Collectibles

Night Drop: A Pinx Video Mystery

IN THE BOYSTOWN MYSTERIES SERIES

The Boystown Prequels

(Little Boy Dead & Little Boy Afraid)

Boystown: Three Nick Nowak Mysteries

Boystown 2: Three More Nick Nowak Mysteries

Boystown 3: Two Nick Nowak Novellas

Boystown 4: A Time for Secrets

Boystown 5: Murder Book

Boystown 6: From the Ashes

Boystown 7: Bloodlines

Boystown 8: The Lies That Bind

Boystown 9: Lucky Days

Boystown 10: Gifts Given

Lambda Award-winning author, Marshall Thornton is known for the best-selling *Boystown* mystery series. Other novels include the erotic comedy *The Perils of Praline, or the Amorous Adventures of a Southern Gentleman in Hollywood*, *Desert Run* and *Femme*. Marshall has an MFA in screenwriting from UCLA, where he received the Carl David Memorial Fellowship and was recognized in the Samuel Goldwyn Writing awards. He is a member of Mystery Writers of America.

CPSIA information can be obtained
at www.ICGtesting.com
Printed in the USA
LVHW030312310821
696470LV00004B/674

9 781983 576201